PATTON BOUNTY HUNTER

Short Story Series

7 Adventures

DEDICATION
This short story and all those that follow that have the fictional bounty hunter Dale Lee Patton are dedicated -

To Grandpa Dale "Pappy" Patton
He was a character!

Kurt James

Colorado Storyteller

Disclaimer

Kurt James

TABLE OF CONTENTS

PATTON BOUNTY HUNTER The Beginning

CHAPTER 1

The snow was getting heavy, but Jeb the dingo forged ahead in front of me breaking trail through four inches of fresh-fallen snow. Realizing I needed to put any thought of the girl Mexican bandit in the back of my mind. Meeting her in Telluride, Colorado was pure and simple luck, she had hopefully given me the information I had been seeking and hunting for the last six months. If what she had told me was true, then Cash Jackson had holed up thirty-one miles away in the town of Ridgway, Colorado for the winter. It would seem that fate and destiny and the possibility of my death awaited me in Ridgway.

Abandoning all thoughts of Lucille the fiery bandit because she would only cloud my judgement and make me confused about the next step in my life to take. As much as I had enjoyed meeting the outlaw Senorita - I needed to forget her for now, I had an oath to fulfill and there was a good possibility I would not survive my coming encounter with Jackson. My hatred for the man that had slaughtered and brutalized my wife had given me a mission and sort of religion. The idea of a final retribution of Jackson consumed every thought I had in the last six months. The thought of killing him had probably destroyed everything that was ever good and righteous in my soul. After finding my wife beaten and dead from the hands of the outlaw burnt a hole all the way through me. I was a burnt-out shell of a man full of thoughts of revenge and justice. My hatred for Jackson gives me strength and drive to keep pushing myself to every known limit of endurance. Hatred and revenge in this case were a wondrous thing for it took that and much more to bring this to a finish - It was my intention to send Jackson straight to hell. I realized that my church upbringing told me for such thoughts of killing the man would find me a seat right along with him beyond the gates of Hades and it was a price I was more than willing to pay. Yes, no way, no how, could I let the engaging dark hair beauty of the Mexican bandit senorita fog my judgement.

Just like the clouds and storm over Mount Sneffels and the San Juan Mountains just to my east my mood darkened some as I realized I may never see a woman that stirred my blood like Senorita Lucille ever again. She had the spitfire and confidence that so reminded of me of my wife Patricia. After meeting Lucile I had a wave of guilt wash over me for having a desire for another woman when my true love in Patricia had been taken from me by Cash Jackson. Meeting the Mexican bandit had confused me some. I had to force myself to leave the petite brown eyed Mexican ball of fire behind. I had not completed my mission to extract justice from Jackson; I had to move on.

So went my mood, so went the weather as the blizzard was intensifying and blowing across the Mount Sneffels above timberline. So far the worst of the storm had stayed higher than the 9000 feet altitude than where I was now, which gave Jeb the dingo, Cinders my mare, and I the window of opportunity to travel from Telluride to Ridgway.

The cold and snow seemed to have no effect on the cinnamon-colored short-haired Australian born dingo Jeb that had become my constant and steadfast companion. Jeb had been given to me by a dying ship captain turned gold prospector over a year ago. I had dogs before-good dogs, but nothing like Jeb. Jeb was the embodiment of a free and natural spirit. He was independent, noble, graceful, dignified, reflective, and had tremendous loyalty to me. Sometimes I wondered who the master was - Jeb or me.

The two days since leaving Telluride had been bitter cold and exhausting and with an almost run in with a starving mountain lion that decide that trying to hunt Cinders, Jeb, and I was not to her liking before moving on to easier game.

It was not long before the town of Ridgway stood before me. Ridgway began as a railroad town, serving the nearby mining towns of Telluride and Ouray. The town site is at the northern terminus of the Rio Grande Southern Railroad where it meets with Denver and Rio Grande Western Railroad running between Montrose and Ouray. Some newspaper back east had called Ridgway the "Gateway to the San Juans" and the phrase had caught on. When you heard "Gateway to the San Juans" anywhere along the Rocky Mountain frontier you knew folks were talking about Ridgway, Colorado.

Looking down into the main street of the town, it did not resemble any gateway to me. It was a town like every other mountain town I had ever come across in my travels through the Rocky Mountains. More saloons than houses and the townsfolk no doubt comprised all walks of life. Store keeps, gamblers, saloon owners, gold miners, cowhands, lawmen, outlaws, churchgoers, and soiled doves lived and tried to make their fortunes here. The good people and the dregs of society walked side by side here on the muddy streets of Ridgway. I was not interested in any of the townsfolk, there was only one man I was interested in and that was Cash Jackson.

Pulling back gently on Cinders my blood bay three-year-old mare's reins I brought her to a halt. Jeb sat his butt down and I could see his panting breath as it danced in the cold mountain air. Slipping off the rawhide thongs from around both of my Smith & Wesson hammer's that held them from falling out of their holsters while on the trail I palmed my right-handed Smith & Wesson Schofield pistol first and then my left-handed one and added a 45 shell to the empty chambers that was usually kept empty for safety. I also checked the loads on my Winchester to make sure it was fully loaded. Even If Jackson was not still here in Ridgway, I wanted to be ready for all encounters.

Looking towards the heaven the sun had finally broken through the clouds just before sunset. As the sun started to finish its arc of the day behind the mountains to the west, I felt several snowflakes land of my cheek and melt. Watching the sunset as it peeked through the clouds and it always amazed me by the magnificence of a high mountain sunset. Feeling the cold of the coming night air I spurred Cinders toward Ridgway.

The livery stable and corral was on the southwestern edge of the town and I thought that was a good place as any to pick up any information if Cash Jackson was wintering here in Ridgway. After unsaddling Cinders, I let her loose in the pole corral with about 10 other horses in it. I paid the livery man with a suspiciously common name of John Smith the going rate plus two dollars more for some extra care for my horse. Mr. Smith when asked if he knew who Cash Jackson was he raised his eyebrows, because he recognized the name, but said nothing. Everyone along this high mountain frontier had heard of Cash Jackson since he was a well-known gunfighter and an outlaw. Trying to get the quiet livery man to talk I asked him if Jackson was possibly in town and once again Mr. Smith played as if he was deaf and dumb. It would seem that Smith was a tad afraid of Jackson and did not want to be known as the man that had pointed him out to a stranger. Cash Jackson spread fear everywhere he went and most folks did not want to make a foe out of such a dangerous man. The only reason the livery man was more afraid of Jackson than myself, because he had yet to get to know me. He did not know that Dale Lee Patton was a man that you did not trifle with. The man that had raised me the mountain man legend himself, Matt Lee had seen to that.

I was half Scottish and half Ute Indian. When I was yet a year old my father, Guy Patton - a mountain man had been killed during a battle with the Arapaho Indians at Grand Lake at the base of Bald Mountain in the Middle Park region of the Never Summer Mountains. My mother was a Ute Indian princess who later married the legendary mountain man Matt Lee. Matt Lee in his younger days had single handily fought the Ute nation to a standstill killing over 20 of their greatest warriors in hand to hand combat before making peace with them after saving my mother from a mountain lion attack. The Ute out of grudging respect for Matt Lee had given him the name "Ghost" and my mother after marrying him took the handle of "Walk With Ghost". When I was 14, I had taken the name Lee as my middle name.

Since I was not getting any information from the closed mouth livery man except for the location of a good hotel I moved on.

Heading down what served as the muddy main street of the town of Ridgway Jeb and I passed several saloons and more than a few drunken cowboys, mountain men and gold miners. I knew this was a rough and rowdy settlement with little or no law and that life was cheap here. All took notice of me and Jeb the dingo. No-one said anything to me, but all kept their eyes on the strange-looking dog by my side.

As the night finally took hold, and the sun disappeared the stars started their nightly dance across the sky and Jeb and I watched them for a spell before heading to the Ridge Hotel to see if they had a room for rent. The Ridge Hotel was a simple one floor rough-hewed cabin affair with 8 rooms. A smaller man with a hawkish nose named Jasper owned the Hotel. Jasper had an easy manner and smile and Jeb seemed to take a shine to him as he trotted right up to the smaller man and flopped over on his back for Jasper to give him a belly rub, which the hotel owner was more than happy to oblige. I did not have to be a Ute Indian to know that was a sign he was a good man.

After paying for the room, Jasper asked if I had eaten yet this evening and finding out I had not set me up with a heaping bowl of beef stew and some Dutch oven biscuits to wipe up the drippings. He even produced several elk bones with generous portions of meat still attached for Jeb to savor on. After polishing off that mighty fine stew and a piece of apple pie, I asked Jasper if he had ever heard of Cash Jackson and if he was in Ridgway. The question momentarily took Jasper by surprise and he looked me in the eye for almost a full minute as he was trying to figure out if I was the law or a friend of the dangerous outlaw. I thought I should clarify that point, "My name is Dale Lee Patton and my Australian dingo hound is Jeb and the truth is I am not the law or a friend of Cash Jackson. I am here to bring to him what he has coming. Plain and simple I am here to take his life. Last June Jackson went on an outlaw rampage through Gunnison and came upon my ranch while I was out seeing to my cattle and after spotting my pretty wife Patricia he could not stop himself from doing unspeakable things to my love. He left her dead and for six grueling months now I have trailed him finally to your town Jasper. My hatred for the man knows no boundaries and I aim to take pleasure in bringing Jackson the reckoning he so deserves."

I could see understanding move across Jasper's face and he nodded his head "yes," before speaking, "Mr. Patton my mother called me an old soul and usually with one glance I know a person's heart. In your eyes I see a haunted man driven by hatred, but in your heart, I feel that you are a good and righteous man that needs to see this damnable crusade to an end. Yes, Mr. Patton the man Cash Jackson is here in town and has been for several weeks now. The sheriff has monitored Jackson, but the man is not wanted here and has done nothing of yet to warrant being arrested. I have to tell you that wherever Jackson goes in town, everyone walks on eggshells around the man. His reputation as a gun hand is on the par with the likes of Johnny Ringo, Wild Bill Hickok, and Lucas Eldridge. I almost feel obligated not to tell you Mr. Patton since I do not want to be responsible for your safety."

Feeling that Jasper was a noble and principled man it humbled me to know such a man as the hotel owner. Smiling as I spoke to calm his fears and reservations, "Jasper, I was hunting Jackson. It would have mattered not if you told me about Cash Jacksons whereabouts or not, destiny and fate is in play here and I would have found him one way or another. I do, however thank you for your concern."

Jasper with a heavy sigh responded, "He is a man that trouble follows and he seems to relish it. The man you seek fancies the Double Eagle Saloon."

After a full meal and two full days of winter trail, I felt more ready for bed than an encounter with Cash Jackson, but I could not take the gamble that he might leave town during the night. Standing slowly with my winter wolf fur cap in my hand, I shaped it somewhat before snapping it back on my head, "If you would be so kind Jasper and point me in the direction of the Double Eagle Saloon I would be much obliged."

Now with no hesitation Jasper said in a clear voice, "You will not need your horse Mr. Patton the Double Eagle Saloon is just about 50 yards down the road to the east on the north side. Jackson always sits at the table with his back to the north wall facing the room and can see all that enters. He will see you enter, there will be no surprise."

Having said that Jasper being the good man that he was - now stuck out his hand to shake mine, "I will build a fire in the fireplace in your room for when you and Jeb's return."

Grabbing my Winchester that had been leaning against the wall next to my seat while eating my supper - Jeb and I headed out the door.

CHAPTER 2

Stepping out onto the front porch of the Ridge Hotel I palmed both of my Schofield's once again to make sure they were fully loaded with six. Holstering both of the Smith & Wesson Scofield's, I then drew both at the same time checking my speed. The Schofield's slid fast and easily into my hands. Holstering them once again, I then jacked the lever on my Winchester to make sure I had a shell in the firing chamber. Now I felt ready for anything that I may encounter this evening.

Jeb was standing by my side and he knew something was up. He was alert to everything around us. I took a full minute standing there feeling the cold winter night air. The recent snow had stopped, and the air was crisp, cold, and smelled of wood fire smoke and evergreens. The clouds above had moved out, and the stars danced their merry lights across the heavens. At this lofty mountain heights one almost could feel they were close enough to reach out and grab a twinkling star. Some felt that autumn was the most beautiful season of the four. It was my thought after the death

9

of autumn every year that winter with all its purity in the way of snowfall was the most beautiful. The evergreens scattered around town were heavy with the recent snow and rustled slightly to the always present mountain breeze. If one listened carefully, you could hear the songs that evergreens sang in in the Rocky Mountain gentle wind. Just as that thought crossed my thinker a couple of snowflakes fluttered by my face and the mellow tone of a piano floated on a draft of wind. Although the piano was not in tune, I recognized the ballad called "Camptown Races."

Stepping off the front porch, I headed east toward the Double Eagle Saloon. The saloon was easy to find since it was the closest saloon on the north side of the road. Once I was on the boardwalk, I stopped for a minute and closed my eyes and took a deep breath. Even before entering I knew the man that had murdered my wife was inside-I felt his presence beyond the doors of the saloon. Having never seen Jackson himself in person I pulled from my vest pocket the Denver newspaper article that had a rendering of his likeness in it and stared at it for a few seconds and burned the image into my mind once again. Being a saloon in the Rocky Mountains it had two sets of doors. One set of full double doors that opened inward that kept the cold and snow on the outside and one set of batwing doors set in front of the double doors for the hot summer days. Jeb and I had to open both sets of doors to enter the Double Eagle Saloon this evening.

A cold sweat trickled between my shoulder blades under my buckskin shirt. The artist for the newspaper that had drawn the picture of Jackson must have been very talented for he seemed to have captured the likeness of the man that had murdered my wife well enough for me to recognize him.

There were four men in the saloon besides myself. The man I believed to be Cash Jackson, a grey-haired bartender with a ponytail and a handlebar mustache that was half asleep, and what looked like two older gold miners that were busy playing cribbage and drinking whiskey to really notice Jeb or myself.

Jasper was correct in that Jackson was sitting just as he had described it. Cash had his back to the north wall with a half full bottle of whiskey in his right hand. He was in the middle of pouring as I walked in and took one look at me before finishing topping off his shot glass. What Jasper did not mention was that he had a 12-gauge Greener double-barrel shotgun laying on top of his table with the barrels pointed toward the front door. It would seem that Jackson was not the trusting type and felt the need to have a show of force sitting on the table in front of him for anyone that may have the courage or the nerve to speak to the outlaw.

If I had been a betting man, I would bet my last dollar it was loaded with double-ought buckshot. He also had a shoulder pistol rig hung on his left shoulder with a Colt 44 in the holster with the grip pointed outward in a cross draw manner. Since he was sitting down, I could not see if he was also armed with a conventional holster.

The saloon smelled of stale tobacco, whiskey and damp sweat. I could even smell the privy out back of the saloon somewhere. Strolling to the bar, but keeping Jackson and the two gold miners in my line of sight, I laid my Winchester on top of the bar pointed not at Jackson, but in his general direction. The sound of laying my weapon on the bar startled and woke up the bartender who asked me, "Well friend what can I get you?"

Not taking my eyes off of Cash and in a level voice, "Whiskey if you have it or a mug of beer if you don't."

The bartender sets a clean shot glass in front and began to fill it with a generous amount of whiskey from a filthy bottle, "That will be 2-bits."

After sliding 4-bits on to the bar, I said in a clear and strong voice, "Sir, I am at the end of a long road so pour me two to celebrate this day."

As I sipped my first drink, I saw my reflection in a mirror hanging behind the bar and what stared back at me was a man I no longer knew. Just as the hotel owner Jasper had said I had the look of a haunted and haggard man. The last six months had taken its toll on my mind and body, I thought I looked older than my 28 years of age. Under my wolf's fur cap I kept my dark hair cut short to keep the critters from making a home in it while in the wilds. Beneath my fringed mountain elk buckskins I weighed somewhere about 200 pounds after losing 20 pounds in the last several months. My 200 pounds were stacked on a 6' 2" frame that was lined with powerful muscle. Living life here in the Rocky Mountains you had to toughen up, or you died. Although worn because of the hunt for the man that had killed Patricia I was as tough as the mountains were old. Cash Jackson may have been a man killer, but what he could not have known was that the ultimate warrior that had raised me was the legendary Matt Lee alias the Ghost.

Even though Cash Jackson had no inkling of who I was or that his life was for me to take. In the calm before the storm I sipped my whiskey, and the memories flooded my thoughts. The early years when Matt Lee became my stepfather and mentor were of learning to survive the hardships of the wilderness and the Rocky Mountains. The Ute Indian legend Ghost had spent my early years teaching me all he knew of nature and the animals that lived in the Rocky Mountains. He had taught me many types of hand to hand combat with guns and knives or fists if it came to that. He taught me that having a killer instinct kept one alive in these hard times. To survive when it mattered you had to put any fear of your own death aside and be willing to die for what you believed in. These lessons handed to me by the mountain man legend were hard to learn, but learned them I did.

Then in a flash loving memories of Patricia rolled over my thoughts of my survival lessons of my youth growing up with Matt Lee. My memory now softened as I remembered how I had fallen so hard for the smallish dark-haired schoolteacher from Gunnison and the love that she showered onto me. Her eyes were mysterious as in they were green, but always with a hint of blue in them. The beginnings of working together to build a ranch and a life for the children we planned on having. I was as happy and content as I ever wanted to be. Life with Patricia had been the best one I could have dreamed of. That all changed on that early June day when Cash Jackson happened across my ranch. Sitting down the first empty shot glass I picked up the second and turned towards Cash Jackson.

Being that my face was a new one in the saloon Jackson out of self-survival had been watching Jeb and me. To a man like him I must have looked like a troublesome mountain man just down from the high country. I looked at the man I would kill straight in the eye and quickly downed my second whiskey. Without taking my eyes off of Jackson I placed the shot glass upside down on the bar signaling to the barkeep I was done drinking. Jackson was starting to get irritated that I was staring at him; Jeb was standing by my side and giving him the ole' stink eye too. Jackson of course did not know me or that I was here to kill him, but he was eyeballing Jeb and myself something fierce. The gears were spinning in his noggin as he tried to remember me or even if he should know who I was.

Cash Jackson was a known man killer and an outlaw and was a wanted man in most places along the Rocky Mountain frontier, but apparently not here in Ridgway. He looked just like the rendering in the newspaper. He was a big man probably 6'3" and weighed 250 pounds. I had heard that he had killed more than once with just his bare hands. He must have been about 40 years-old with shoulder length dark hair streaked with gray under a black cowboy hat with a cattleman's crease. I could see a red flannel shirt that sported polished bone buttons under an ebony leather vest. His face was clean shaven just like the picture in the paper. Since he was now glaring back at me, I got a good look at his eyes this time and saw the evil that lived within the man. His eye pupils were dark and almost black, I had never seen such eyes before. Outside the pupils they were a dirty milky white. I imagine that most folks would shy away from Jackson when he just gave them one look. I feared no man, especially Cash Jackson and on this day I almost felt pity for the man for he did not understand what awaited him - almost. On this day, Cash Jackson's retribution was coming and he would pay the price for all the murders, robberies, and fear that he had spread where ever he traveled across the Rocky Mountain frontier. Any pity I might have felt for the man had turned to loathing when another flash of Patricia's half-clothed body flashed through my brainpan. Cash Jackson and my fate and what would come was now in play and one if not both of us would die here in Ridgway today.

Keeping my hands free so as to not to impede the time when I drew my weapons, Jackson spoke first, "Do you and that flea bag dog have a problem with me, boy? I don't reckon you are giving me the eye because of me being so handsome."

My mind focused on all that surrounded me at this exact moment in time. I could smell the whiskey in the shot glasses and the staleness of tobacco smoke that lingered in the air. I could hear and feel the stillness of the room as the bartender and the two gold miner cribbage players stopped what they were doing after feeling the tension mount in the stuffy and closed room. Knowing what I read about Jackson the Colt pistol in his shoulder rig would not be his weapon of choice in this close up battle, but rather that Greener double barrel 12-gauge sitting in front of him on the table. I could see in his eyes, he was confident in his ability to use that weapon against me. The killer instinct within me stood up front and center and the fear of my death disappeared into the back corners of my mind. After 6 long months the moment was now, and I was willing and ready to deal the final card and play the hand to the end. I just knew that Jackson had no chance. All that mattered now was the timing. I could hear the tick tock of the clock behind the bar and out of my sight. Little did Cash Jackson know that the clock was now counting down the last final minutes of his life!

Not knowing he only had a few ticks of the clock left to live Jackson spoke again, actually he almost growled as he said, "I will ask you just once more son. Do you and that mangy dog have a problem with me?"

With a smirk on my face and in a confident voice, "I see you are struggling Cash in trying to recall if you know me or not. You do not, but I know you. Let me ask you a question. Do you remember a small ranch west of Gunnison on the trail to the Black Canyon?"

Jackson face went blank for a tad, then a smile spread across his face as he spoke, "The one-room cabin with the white picket fence out front?"

Spreading my feet so they were directly under my shoulders in a gunfighter's stance, I held back the hatred for the man since I had to think and react naturally. Anger can cloud the mind and I pushed it all the way back so my thinker was clear. Still in a loud and clear voice with no hesitation, I answered Jackson's question, "One and the same. I want you to see the man up close that is here to take your life Jackson! I am that man!"

"You speak boldly for a skinny no-account kid still wet behind the ears, must be that grungy looking dog that gives you courage. What are you, some wannabe bounty hunter looking to get killed by one of his betters?"

My face showed no expression when I spoke next, "Not a bounty hunter, just a husband to exact justice from the man who butchered his wife."

The smile quickly evaporated off Jackson's face as he moved swiftly towards his shotgun in front of him. As Ghost had taught me I palmed my Smith & Wessons with lightning speed. Jackson's eyebrows raised as he saw the speed in which I drew both of my weapons - he had not counted on that.

Firing once from each Smith & Wesson with the bullets catching Jackson in his throat at almost the same instance. With the advent of the bullets punching a gaping hole in his throat, then out the back Cash instinctively stopped reaching for the shotgun and his hands flew to his throat trying to stem his life blood from flowing. His attempt to staunch the flow was to no avail. His life was squirting through his fingers. Holstering my left Schofield, I walked closer so he could get a good look at the man that had killed him, Jackson was still alive and his eyes were wide open when I spoke, "Six months I trailed you Cash for this very moment. Today is the first day for the rest of eternity that you will spend in hell! This is for Patricia!" Raising my right pistol again, I fired a second time placing a nice round hole in his forehead. The momentum of the last shot sent the man that had slaughtered my wife slamming into the wall behind him and his legs kicked out knocking the table over dumping the Greener shotgun on the floor. Jackson was still holding his throat, but very much a dead man as his body did a slow slide down the wall into a growing puddle of his blood on the floor.

Jeb the dingo had been standing by my side the whole time content to let me handle the situation. Seeing Cash Jackson down the Australian mutt paid a tribute the only way Jeb could, and he promptly walked up and lifted his leg and peed on the now cooling body of the dead renegade.

Looking at the man that I had just killed and knowing there was no man more deserving of dying a violent death than Cash Jackson, I felt - nothing! No happiness like I thought I would have nor did I feel remorse - I felt nothing at all! No sense of accomplishment. Justice had been done, revenge had been done, justice had been dealt, but Patricia was still dead. It was like all the innocence of my youth had been sapped out of me the day my wife died.

I quickly reloaded out of habit other than thinking about it and then holstered both of my pistols. Righting the table and then pulling up a chair from the table that Cash Jackson lay dead next to I sat down hard and waited for the law to show up. I knew from seeing previous gunfights in towns across the Colorado Rockies that it would not take long for the townsfolk and their lawman to make an appearance. Looking at Jeb then tapping my right leg Jeb leaped into my lap and he comforted me as I petted him thinking about all that had just happened and then what I should do next.

The sheriff of Ridgway was a no-nonsense, very large man and had the look of a man that could handle himself in any situation. Once he had heard my side of the story and how Jackson had murdered my wife and the barkeep and the two gold miners vouched that my retelling of the righteous shooting was an accurate account the sheriff seemed relieved that he did not have to arrest me for getting rid of a man such as Cash Jackson from his town and jurisdiction. After writing and signing the paperwork involved in such a lawful killing, he said something that I had never even thought of, "Mr. Patton even though Jackson was not a wanted man here, there is a substantial dead or alive bounty from where he is a wanted man. No one here, including myself wanted to go up against a man such as Cash Jackson. You will have to stay in town for a few days will I wire for and to receive the $2000 cash bounty you have coming. That should make it easier to start up again on your ranch near Gunnison."

A $2000 bounty? It had never even crossed my mind that by killing Cash Jackson that I would make that kind of money. That is not why I did what I did. I had killed Jackson for the justice and revenge - nothing more. There was no doubt I needed the money since I had spent all I could scrape together in my pursuit of Jackson. Going back to my ranch no longer appealed to me, because my life there west of Gunnison had vanished into the mountain mist the day Patricia died. The sheriff looked to me as if he expected me to say something and once I had it sorted out some in my mind, I spoke, and "The day my wife died changed my life forever sheriff. I will not be going back to what is left of my ranch in Gunnison."

With nowhere in particular to go and now with time on my hands, I said in a clear voice, "While waiting for the bounty money to be delivered sheriff I think I will take that time going through all of your wanted posters. Especially the dead or alive posters with the highest bounty awards."

Kurt James

PATTON BOUNTY HUNTER 2nd Adventure

CHAPTER 1

The day was warm, and I was riding against the wind on this early summer day just at timberline. Cinders, my mare stumbled as a rock rolled under her hoof which made Thomas Legit's horse stumble since I had tethered his mare to my saddle by its reins. Once Cinders righted her footing, I pulled back on her reins and brought her to a halt. Looking behind me at Thomas Legit I wanted to make sure the stumble hadn't caused the outlaw's body to slide into a position to fall off his horse. Legit was a big man, and it took everything I had to pick him up and put him cross ways over his saddle, and I sure did not want him falling off and having that struggle all over again.

Thomas Legit had been a wanted man along the Rocky Mountain frontier and the $250 bounty was more than enough to warrant the effort on my part to track him down. The wanted poster said dead or alive and Mr. Legit had not been inclined to come peacefully when Jeb my Australian dingo and I came upon his prospecting campsite 4 miles west of Kokomo, Colorado. He fast palmed his Colt pistol, but was no match for me and my brace of Scofield 45's. Since we were close to Kokomo and I sort of knew the lawman, so I decided to turn his body over to Sheriff Pat Buckley in Kokomo and put a claim in on the bounty from there.

Once reaching the outskirts on the northern edge of Kokomo I halted Cinders and took a long pull from my canteen as I surveyed the town just below me. Jeb sat his butt down as he also took a breather and seemed for the moment content in surveying the town with me as a good partner would.

Kokomo was the center of activity in what has come to be known as the Tenmile District. The Kokomo-Tenmile district is an irregularly shaped area of about 45 square miles, located in parts of Summit, Eagle, and Lake Counties, in the central mountains of Colorado. The Kokomo mining settlement sprang up after they made a few placers gold discoveries. They had named the settlement after a town in Indiana and was not much to write home about until the discovery of silver ore. Once the silver boom started the town grew, and it was said to have upwards of 10,000 people living here and the surrounding mountains.

Although a growing town - it also experienced the lawlessness typical of mining boom towns. Whiskey and soiled doves were expensive, but life was cheap in such towns. I always had to be careful and grow an extra set of eyes in these mining boom towns, for there were always young guns that were out to make a name for themselves as a gunfighter. All these youngsters had heard the tales of the gunfighter turned bounty hunter-Dale Lee Patton. Some folks talked as if I had become a legend almost on par with the man that had raised me the famous mountain man Matt Lee. The status as a gunfighter and or having the reputation of a legend was nothing I needed or wanted. This gunfighter reputation had been thrust on me after 6 months of tracking down and killing the outlaw, renegade Cash Jackson the man that had killed my wife Patricia. It was after her murder I had lost all interest of settling down on a ranch and raising a family and I decided to do what it seemed I had more than enough skill for and I became a bounty hunter.

Once I had quenched my thirst, I gave Cinders the reins and her head and a slight jab of my right spur and we moved out slowly until we reached the main street of Kokomo. Not much of a street, more like a muddy mess from the recent mountain showers. The town had more than a few folks out and about and just like every mining boom town you had all walks of life from gamblers, Orientals, miners, cowpokes, saloon owners, dance hall girls, but there was only one man in town that I was interested in and that was the local lawman and an acquaintance of mine the sheriff Pat Buckley. The one man that can help me put in a claim on the $250 bounty.

Kokomo had its fair share of wood-framed boardwalks and buildings with murky broad glass for windows, but it was also a town of many merchants set up in canvas tents. I had been here once before and it seemed the settlement had grown twice as large since that visit. At no time of all I was able to locate the sheriff's office and Pat Buckley was standing outside leaning against an awning post smoking a hand-rolled cigar. Buckley was a big man with narrow hips and he had a reputation of a man not only good with his Colt pistol strapped to his right leg, but also as a hard nose and dangerous man with his fists. He enforced the law as he saw fit in Kokomo. Pat smiled when he saw Jeb and I and while he was still smoking his foul smelling cigar he said, "Well, it would seem since you are hauling what looks to be a dead body Patton are you here to report a death or claim a reward. Which one is it?"

After bringing Cinders and Jeb to a halt in front of the sheriff I step down out of the saddle and wrapped the reins around the closest hitching post and replied, "The bounty sheriff, this is Thomas Legit and he is wanted in Teller County."

Sheriff Buckley snubbed out his cigar and stepped off the boardwalk and lifted Legit's head and study it for a moment before speaking, "This hombre has been around Kokomo for several weeks, never checked the wanted posters to see if he was a wanted man though."

After comparing Legit to the wanted posted that I had, Sheriff Buckley then filled out the paperwork that was needed to claim the reward money. We then went next door to the telegraph office where the sheriff wired for the $250 bounty from Teller County, where Legit had been wanted for murder and bank robbery.

Sitting across from the sheriff's desk, I thumbed through the wanted posters he had stacked so neatly on the top of his desk and came across one that caught my eye since it had a substantial award printed on the bottom. One for $1000.

Reading the poster twice and then I lowered it down so Jeb the dingo could read it who cocked his head to the side in confusion reminding me my partner was just a dog. Laughing I rubbed him behind his right ear the way he liked it and then I spoke to Jeb, "I was just wondering if you had an objection to us going after one of your kind you mangy mutt!"

Jeb stood and wagged his tail something fierce and barked twice, which I took as he didn't care who we went after. Still smiling at Jeb I slid the wanted poster for 3 Toes the gray wolf across the desk towards the sheriff and asked, "What's the story about this wolf?"

Sheriff Buckley picked up the wanted poster and after reading it, he said, "Patton that bounty may be the toughest job you have ever had. 3 Toes has become legendary in these parts since he has been killing livestock in these mountains and the high meadows and pastures for over 15 years, some ranchers in those counties started calling the wolf 3 Toes from his very distinctive track of only having 3 toes just like the rendering on the poster. Some speculate that he must have lost a toe to a jump trap at some time in his life. Some wolf hunters have followed his 3-toed tracks in a 200-mile circle without ever getting even one sighting of the mystical beast. The Ute Indians believe 3 Toes has supernatural abilities which gives him the skill to elude his pursuers. Every bounty hunter, Indian, rancher that have tried to track 3 Toes down has been baffled - these tough and mountain bred men that had tried to hunt down 3 Toes have been the most experience trackers in the Rocky Mountains and yet they have not even spotted the ghost wolf. It would seem the renegade wolf is one of the most intelligent and cunning outlaw wolf that anyone has ever encountered."

The sheriff slid the wanted poster back across the desk in my direction. Picking it up I looked again at the $1000 bounty and said, "One thousand dollars for a wolf is a lot of money. Who is backing that kind of money for the bounty?"

Sheriff Buckley cleared his throat before replying to my question, "A cattle rancher named Vincent Moore originally from Canada now owns the biggest cattle spread in Summit County, he also owns the Winning Card silver mine. Moore has accumulated a lot of land and has become wealthy enough to be called Mr. Moore. He claims that 3 Toes is not only killing for food, but just for the thrill of killing. Other ranchers in the area feel the same way. Some even think the killer wolf is the spawn of the devil since it seems to be unstoppable in its killing spree. Mr. Moore has even more incentive to have the wolf killed than most. Just over a year ago 3 Toes had maimed and killed his 7-year-old grandson while on his way to the privy one night."

Hearing about the death of the young boy was the deciding factor if Jeb and I would try to track down the wolf. It hit home with me the grief that Vincent Moore and his family must have felt with such a savage death of the young lad. After losing my wife and any chance of having children of my own with her when she had been murdered by an outlaw - I felt the need to bring some closure to the Moore family for the tragic death of one of theirs. Reaching down, I gave Jeb a good ruffling on his head and then I looked at the sheriff, "I reckon Jeb and I are going for 3 Toes and the bounty. Do you have any idea if there have been any recent attacks so we might pick up his trail?"

CHAPTER 2

Sheriff Buckley reached into a stack of papers on his desk and pulled out a telegraph dispatch and read it to himself before answering my question, "Just had a wire from Breckenridge this morning stating 3 Toes just yesterday slaughtered 3 yearling calves down near the Blue River just outside of Breckenridge on the Ford Gulch Ranch near the Country Boy Mine. The wire also mentions the calves had been barely feasted upon and seems that they had been killed just for the pleasure of killing. Patton this wolf is an intelligent, cunning, dangerous, and a man killer - Dale you better ride with your nose to the wind and your eyes to the shadows when tracking such a foe."

Taking in what the sheriff said and pondering about it for a spell before I asked another question, "Ford Gulch Ranch, is that the same one owned by Russell Ford? If so, I am familiar with that area."

Pat Buckley indicated with a "yes" nod of his head that it was one and the same. Picking up the wanted poster on the killer wolf I bid the sheriff good bye and Jeb and I headed out the door of his office. Once in the saddle on Cinders, I pulled her around and gave her a slight jab of my right spur as we moved out towards the town of Breckenridge and the Blue River. Jeb was eager for the trail and he took the lead as if he was the ramrod of the outfit. He probably was and he just hadn't let me in on it yet.

After the riding the trail to Breckenridge the sun was almost finishing its daily arc and was dropping below the mountains in the west with the most spectacular sunset of blue and orange. Pulling back on Cinders reins I brought her to a halt and the three of us Cinder, Jeb, and myself, then took a few minutes to watch the Lord's mighty fine creation of a perfect Rocky Mountain sunset. For over 28 years every day I have watched the sunrise and sunset here, along the "Great Divide" and felt blessed to live where only others can dream about. I have never seen the Smokey Mountains back east, but felt that they were only ant hills compared to my Rocky Mountains. My step-father the legendary mountain man that raised me from the young pup I was into the man I am today taught me the ways of the mountains. The big lesson, of course, was you can never master the wilderness since it has a 100 different ways it can kill you. You learned to live with nature and the wild and not to fight it. It was a lesson I had learned well.

Since it was late and darkness was not far off, which would make it difficult to pick up the trail of 3 Toes, I headed down the muddy and rutted road that served as the main street of Breckenridge and located a livery stable to board Cinders for the night and then headed to the Gold Pan saloon and hotel for supper and a bed for Jeb and me. The worn and older woman that served as the waitress in the café side of the saloon was as busy as a small dog in tall oats as she moved quickly from table to table serving up the special of the day which was - fried tatters and venison steak with a slice of apple pie. As soon as I sat down at an old rickety wooden table, the woman dropped a plate in front of me with a warm beer. Jeb jumped up on the seat next to me and was eyeballing the steak as much as I was. We both were as hungry as if we had tapeworms hollering for fodder. After waving down the waitress I pointed at the dingo and showed her I needed another plate for Jeb and she gave me the ole' stink eye, but went and fetched one. After sharing about a third of my supper including a slice of my apple pie with Jeb which seemed more than fair since I was a lot bigger than he was.

Both Jeb and I were contented with our bellies full when we retreated to our room without stopping at the bar. I was not in the mood tonight to deal with a passel of drunken miners and ranch hands, plus I wanted to get an early start in the morning for the Ford Gulch Ranch the scene of the latest attack and slaughter by the ghost wolf 3 Toes.

Waking up an hour before the sun I was drenched with sweat. The reoccurring dream of the day I found Patricia my wife butchered by Cash Jackson had spent most of the night swimming around in my thinker. Although I had tracked the outlaw down and Cash Jackson was now dead, the aftermath of what he did to my wife has never left me - and to this day still haunts me.

Standing slowly as not to disturb my cinnamon-colored dingo, for nightmares did not trouble him and he was sleeping soundly on the bed where he had spent the night with me. I moved to the dresser that held the pitcher of water and the wash basin and poured a generous amount of water into the porcelain bowl and splashed water on my face to clear the cobwebs of sleep and the visions of Patricia laying all exposed and dead on the floor in our cabin near Gunnison, Colorado. Blinking my eyes to clear the water I looked at myself in the mirror hanging on the wall above the dresser and looked at my reflection. What looked back at me was a man that was 28 years-old going on 50. Although women found me to be a handsome man I could not see that in the reflection in the mirror. I thought I looked haggard and haunted. I had dark circles ringing my dark brown eyes that were brought on by the sleepless nights replaying the death of Patricia in my mind night after night. My dark brown hair was cut short, and I had several days' worth of whiskers sprouting on my face. I had slept in my blue flannel shirt and Levi jeans, both of which hung loosely on my 6' 2" tall and heavily muscled body. My face may have the look of a preoccupied man, but my body was hardened and chiseled from living life in these high mountains and along the Rocky Mountain frontier. After washing my face to clear my nightly haunts I felt ready for the day and looked at Jeb and said, "Time for you my lazy mutt to get your butt out of bed. We have a wolf to track."

After a filling breakfast of chicken eggs and elk sausage mopped up with butter biscuits in the café of the Gold Pan saloon and hotel Jeb and I fetched Cinders from the livery stable and made our way east towards the Blue River and the Ford Gulch Ranch.

By mid-morning we had located the ranch and the owner, Russell Ford himself took us to the high meadow where his yearling calves had been butchered. It didn't take a tracker of any ability to see what had happened to the 3 yearlings. There were only the tracks of a lone wolf and the right paw showed who the culprit was. The 3 Toe right paw pad told me this was the work of the ghost like wolf 3 Toes. Putting my hand over the wolf's print without touching it, I had to spread my fingers as wide as I could to cover the print - 3 toes not only was a cunning and dangerous foe - he was huge. As soon as I lifted my hand from the paw print Jeb sniffed the wolf's track and the hackles on his back raised and he let loose that dingo low and menacing growl of his. Looking at Jeb I spoke to him, "You sense it as well my Australian friend that this wolf differs from other wolves. He has got to be close to 175 pounds and does not run with a pack. He is a loner, which makes him more unpredictable than other wolves. Wolves normally do not hunt alone; wondering why this one does is a question for the ages."

Answering the best that he could Jeb put his two cents in and growled and barked twice which meant—hell, I was not sure what that meant but the dingo seemed to be ready for any future encounter with 3 Toes. After replying to me he went back to sniffing the paw prints and the dead yearling calves to get the predators scent. In this hunt I would need Jeb's Australian outback dingo keen ability to smell as with his superior flair to hear and see better than I could. He was my partner and I could tell by his reaction to this kill site he was all in and ready for the hunt of the ghost like wolf.

Once Russell Ford realized who I was the owner of the Ford Gulch ranch was more than eager to outfit Jeb and I with supplies to begin the hunt of the killer wolf. His thought was since Vincent Moore was backing the $1000 bounty he could foot the cost of some supplies to one that had such a reputation as a bounty hunter such as myself. I tried to pay for the supplies, but Mr. Ford was having none of it and acted insulted when I tried to pay him in gold.

CHAPTER 3

It was just a tad past midday when Jeb and I began to follow the scent of 3 Toes. Relying on Jeb's ability to track the ghost wolf's scent by mid-afternoon we had already bypassed the gold digs of the Country Boy Mine and moved into the dark timber heading more east than north towards Glacier Peak. Most wolves were predictable in that they were like most critters and they would follow the easiest route along rivers and the base of the mountains. In the beginning of this hunt 3 Toes was proving just as I suspected-that he was anything but a normal wolf since he was heading into the high mountains moving quickly across almost impassable territory.

Although 3 Toes was not shying away from difficult terrain as he headed almost straight for Glacier Peak, which topped out several thousand feet above timberline, common sense told me he would not venture above to those lofty heights. The ghost wolf was the ultimate predator and there would be nothing for him to prey upon where the trees never grew. Jeb was a muscular and strong dingo, but following 3 Toes was proving to be difficult and demanding on my Australian dog, but it would seem that Jeb was not only suited for the task - he was also eager to hunt the wolf. Although 3 Toes had to be 6 times larger than Jeb, the wolf seemed to effortlessly move through the dark timber over and under fallen trees and what not. Jeb was doing all he could do just to follow the scent. Cinders and I would search out the easiest path through the evergreens and aspens and several times we would lose sight of Jeb. Jeb as I had trained him in those occurrences when following the scent where Cinders and I could not follow he would let out a yelp from time to time to give me notice of his location. My face had already gathered several new cuts from tree limbs slapping me as the ghost wolf took us through heavy timber. The thought crossed my mind that 3 Toes knew we were tracking him and was playing us for fools and was punishing us for being chumps for tracking him. Just the idea that a wolf may have the reckoning to think in those terms was almost scary.

At mid-morning on the third day after leaving the Ford Gulch Ranch and with Glacier Peak just to the south of our position 3 Toes changed course. He was now headed more north than east towards the mining camp of Montezuma along the Snake River. We had not stumbled along any kills sites since the 3 yearlings that had been slaughtered and I had a feeling that the elusive killer wolf was getting hungry. It seemed that the killer wolf was heading for some easy grub along the meadows of the Snake River that more than likely had a few ranchers raising cattle to help feed the miners and the townsfolk of Montezuma.

At midday on top of a crest of a mountain that I now found myself, I called for Jeb to a halt and pulled back slightly on Cinders reins to bring her to a stop. Retrieving the Italian Ignazio Porro designed binoculars from my saddle bags that my mentor Matt Lee had given me years ago I study all that was down below me. I surveyed the Snake River that meandered north to south in the high mountain meadow along the river. I could make out several gold panning prospector camps along the river, but what caught my eye was the flock of blackbirds circling around and around in one location northeast of me.

From this distance the birds had to be larger than sparrows for me to be able to see them. They probably were magpies or crows, both of which were scavenger birds. With so many birds present in one locale would indicate that they were feeding or trying to feed on something that had recently died or had been killed. It was my best guess that 3 Toes scent would bring Jeb, Cinders, and I to his latest kill right below the circling black birds.

Jeb had been watching me panting with his tongue hanging out in anticipation of my signal to move out; swinging my hand forward to show he was to start tracking again Jeb moved quickly down the mountainside. After giving Cinders her head and loose reins, she moved out following the dingo.

The scent that Jeb was following brought us to the west side of the Snake River 3 miles south of the mining camp of Montezuma. This time the victim was a Hereford bull; it was almost disturbing that a lone wolf could down and kill what looked to be a healthy and mature bull. As Jeb ran back and forth over the kill site using his nose for the clues of what went on here during the attack, I rode Cinders slowly around the bull as magpies were tearing flesh from the carcass. It was clear that 3 Toes had crippled the large bull first by ripping and tearing below its knees and above the hooves on both rear legs. Having downed the bull the marauding wolf attacked the hamstrings to cripple it even further. Once the bull had no way to defend itself, then 3 Toes feasted on the still dying bull.

Dismounting and after waving my arms scaring off several magpies, I crouched Indian style and looked more closely at the wolf tracks. The 3 toed tracks of the killer wolf were clear and fresh. The wind or weather had yet to wear down the track, and it was my thought this Hereford bull kill was less than a half of a day old.

Jeb had stopped his scurrying and now was pointed almost due east. Off the tip of the dingo's nose I followed with my eyes in the direction he was looking and in the distance I could see Santa Fe Peak. Now looking far I brought my sight in closer down the mountainside and the aspen and evergreen trees back onto the meadow all the way back to Jeb. Jeb hackles were fully standing straight up and then the hair on my arms raised. Jeb felt it first, then I felt it - 3 Toes was close, and he was watching us. We couldn't see him since he was too cunning for that, but both of us felt him.

Knowing the demon wolf was close I decided to see if he might make a mistake and we would get a glimpse of him. Raising my binoculars I focused in on the shadows beneath the evergreens that Jeb was staring at. After several minutes of concentration on my part I saw movement as if a shadow had shifted. Now looking directly at the place of the movement I saw a quick flash of gray fur as 3 Toes turned his attention from us and moved back further into the shadows. The crafty bastard had been watching us.

Still looking east into the dark timber I pulled my canteen from my saddlebag. After taking a long drink of stale water I cupped my hand and gave Cinders a taste to wet her whistle, then bent down and did the same for Jeb. The whole time I was trying to map out our next move. I think we came upon 3 Toes before he had his fill of meat from the bull he had killed and if we had not come upon this kill he would more than likely return here to feast more on the Hereford bull.

Running it through my thinker, I reckoned I had 2 options. First one was wolves were known to come back to a kill site time and time again to feed-so one choice was to ambush him here once he came back to feed again. Then there was a strong possibility that Jeb and I just by being here and leaving our scent next to the dead bull had ruined any chance that the this wolf would come back here ever again. If that was true the only remaining and 2nd option was to stay on the trail of the wolf knowing he was close and hopefully get close enough to be able to pick him off with my Winchester.

Putting my canteen away in the saddle bag I looked at the dingo as if he could read my mind and said, "Well partner, do we stay and try to ambush the wolf or go after him?"

Jeb didn't even think about it for one second and he sprinted eastward towards the dark timber where I had caught a glimpse of 3 Toes. Stepping into the stirrup I quickly planted my butt in the saddle and gave Cinders her head and some spur and we trotted after the Australian dingo.

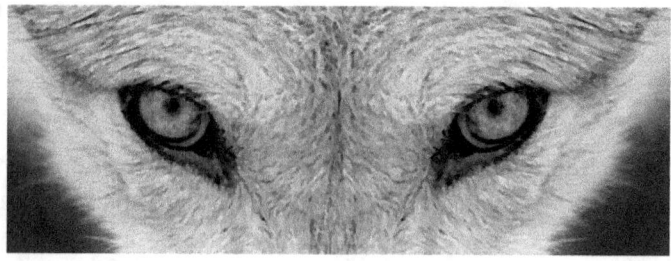

CHAPTER 4

Jeb once he came to the edge between the meadow and the forest of evergreen and aspen trees he stopped and waited for Cinders and me to catch up. Jeb was smart enough to know he would not survive an encounter with the ghost like lone wolf on his own. He knew we needed each other to defeat such a wily and dangerous foe. Once Cinders and I reached the line of trees, I motion my right hand forward showing the dingo to keep tracking. Jeb moved into the dark timber, but more cautiously just as Cinders and I would.

After an hour of trailing through the timber the day was quickly coming to an end as the sun started to drop below the western horizon. Knowing Jeb could follow the scent in the dark I knew it was not wise to hunt and try to take the wolf in the dark. Jeb, Cinders, or I could end up seriously hurt of dead in doing so. Looking to the sky and judging how much light we still had I spoke to Jeb, "Jeb, we need to stop for the night."

Jeb halted, but lurched forward several times trying to encourage me to keep going, "No Jeb, it is too dangerous in the dark. We need to set up camp for the night and we will pick up 3 Toes trail in the morning."

Locating a suitable campsite with a small brook seeping from the mountainside for freshwater I dismounted and began to set up a camp. Jeb reluctantly moved to my side, but kept his eyes darting into the timber in the direction that the killer wolf had gone.

At first I decided to have a cold camp with no fire, but my gut instinct told me I needed one tonight not for warmth or to cook my supper, but to help keep 3 Toes from coming into the camp as we slept. Wolves mostly were just like all wild critters and feared fire. Tonight I thought it wise to keep a fire burning just in case the devious wolf doubled back on us and try to make Cinders or Jeb a meal.

Darkness was falling fast, and I got the fire going before seeing that Cinders needs had been taken care of which was not my normal routine. I was taught by my step-father the mountain man Matt Lee to take care of the horses first above all else. Tonight the fire came first I could feel the presence of the murdering wolf not far off and it might help in keeping him there and out our camp for the night.

After unsaddling Cinders, I gave her a good going over with my wooden curry comb, paying a lot of attention to her mane and tail since both had been snarled with evergreen needles from riding so close to the evergreen tree limbs. Once I had her looking beautiful and feeling sassy, I fed her some grain and a wee bit of sugar for a treat. I was not one for hobbling horses and usually let them move about at night looking for the best grass, but tonight I hobbled Cinders closer to the fire than I was accustomed to. I didn't want her moving too far from Jeb and I in case 3 Toes was out and about our camp tonight. As I groomed Cinders, I had the uneasy feeling that I was being watched and several times I looked into the darkness trying to catch the movement of gray fur or a shadow that shouldn't be there. I palmed both of my Scofield 45's checking my speed. Both slid into my hands with quickness and rapidity. In doing so, I wondered if I would be fast enough if 3 Toes charged me in the dark. I feared no man or wild animal, but I was wary of this wolf. So far he acted like no wolf I had ever encountered before.

With Jeb by my side like the good watch dog he was I gathered more firewood that was scattered here and there around my campsite. My plan was to keep the fire going all night if possible. After adding 2 more sizable logs to the fire, I decided since I had a cook fire I might as well have a warm supper. Going through my grub sack I retrieved 6 chicken eggs, fat-backed bacon, and some tortillas Russell Ford cook had made for me and decided Jeb and I would have a grand supper this evening.

As I was preparing Jeb's and my supper Jeb moved about the camp and he would stare into the darkness in different directions for several minutes at a time. The dingo was nervous, which was making me nervy. He remained close to the fire, but always moving back and forth looking into the night. Jeb was alert and on edge, but Cinders remained calm as she grazed on some tall grass and paid no mind to Jeb or what was out in the night's dark. I was somewhat baffled at Jeb and Cinders different reactions of the night. I was not sure if Jeb was just reacting to 3 Toes scent from today that still lingered since we were on his trail or it was possible I guess that the ghost like wolf was circling our camp and studying us just far enough out of range to not alert Cinders, but close enough to keep Jeb scurrying about our camp. My gut instinct was telling me that 3 Toes was close and this would be a restless night. There was a sinking feeling in my gut that Jeb and I were not the hunters anymore and we now had become the hunted.

After finishing supper I readied all my weapons by cleaning them and making sure that they were fully loaded. My Scofield 45's were looked at first since they would be my weapons of choice in close quarters, then I honed and sharpened my 12 inch Bowie knife in case somehow 3 Toes had gotten in close enough that I would have to fight him by hand. Then last of all was my Winchester for hopefully that far away shot to pick off the killer wolf.

While cleaning my weapons Jeb was sitting so close to me he was touching my leg with his body as his eyes darted about following unforeseen things in the forest. The wild side of my dingo was assuredly feeling the presence of the wolf at close quarters. How close was up for speculation since Cinders as yet had not sensed danger or the wolf. Although I could not see, hear, or smell 3 Toes the hair standing up on my arms told me that the cunning wolf was out there and he was watching and waiting for us to make a mistake. For a lone wolf to stalk a full-grown man, a horse, and a dog all at the same time was a little unsettling. I could not make the mistake that this killer wolf was just an ordinary critter-it would seem he had more smarts than most men that I had tracked. It was obvious that 3 Toes did not fear us and it would seem he feared nothing at all.

As the night grew longer, the stars above danced to an unheard melody of the heavens and twinkled their light down upon us. The half-moon also brought enough light to the night to make the shadows long and somewhat eerie looking. Jeb had finally laid down by my side, but he was not asleep. His ears were standing straight up and twitched to the sounds that only he could hear. I was getting sleepy and my eyelids grew heavy as the night wore on. Trying to stay awake and alert I threw 2 more logs onto the fire and watched the embers float and dance in the heated air rising from the fire. If not for the fact that there was a man killing wolf out in the dark I would have enjoyed this Rocky Mountain evening and would have fallen to sleep easily. The moon rose slowly in the night sky until it was directly overhead. There was a cool northern breeze that carried the smell of pine across the camp. Listening to the hoot of a faraway owl to try to stay awake - didn't work.

My eyes snapped open when Cinders snorted loudly and with fright and started to pound the ground with her front hooves. Although still half asleep, I instinctively palmed my right-handed Scofield as I tried quickly to gain my feet. I had fallen asleep and now my thinker was now trying to catch up to what was happening. Looking to Cinders while she was panic stricken, I was trying to piece together what the hell was going on. I saw her eyes wide with terror as she looked due east. Following her gaze quickly I saw a large shadow move just beyond the light of the campfire. It was 3 Toes, and he had Jeb's head in his jaws and was jerking his body back and forth trying to break the dingo's neck. Firing on instinct at the killer wolf I heard the bullet slam home into his body.

Shooting the wolf didn't drop him or even slow him down and all it seemed to do was piss him off as he violently slung Jeb's body to the side as 3 Toes turned to face me the new adversary. Knowing now I did not have to fear accidently shooting Jeb I fired again as the wolf started to lunge in my direction. Once again, I heard the thud of the 45 as it slammed home into the body of the fast closing wolf. With two slugs in him 3 Toes now leaped over the fire and I fired a third round into him just before feeling the full impact of the 175 pound wolf as he slammed into my body. My right-hand pistol went flying off into the darkness as I tumbled backwards trying to hold off 3 Toes as he was snapping at my throat with my now empty right hand. Jamming my forearm into the wolf's mouth and pushing with all my strength I was gaging the ghost wolf and keeping him from getting a full bite on my arm, but his teeth had punctured my buckskin shirt and the meat below it. The taste of blood sent 3 Toes into a maddening fury as I was able to with my left hand pull my Bowie knife from the scabbard on my left side. With my right forearm still within his jaws and with all my strength with my left arm I stabbed the wolf from hell through his ribcage as he was still savagely trying to rip my arm off. Feeling the wolf's blood wash over my hand, I stirred the knife, hoping to nick the savage beast's heart. Pulling the knife out of his body, I quickly stabbed 3 more times before feeling 3 Toes powerful jaws slackening on my right forearm. Looking into 3 Toes eyes, I could see the devil himself lived beyond the eyes of this hound from hell, I also saw his mortal life fading and sputtering as we both slumped to the ground. On my knees I pulled my right forearm free, and the blood started flowing from my wounded arm and I was now covered in crimson from both 3 Toes and myself.

With more effort than I had strength for I disengaged myself from the dying wolf and stood shaking on my 2 feet. Lightheaded from the fight and probably blood loss I looked at my foe that had probably killed my dog and almost killed me. In the dying light of the campfire I could see the Satan's wolf was still alive, and he was trying to stand and his death snarl had returned. This wolf had been shot at close range 3 times and stabbed 4 times and was looking like he was gathering his strength to take another run at me. Not thinking I wanted any more of what 3 Toes had just dished out I dropped my Bowie knife and fast palmed my left-handed Scofield and said, "This is for Jeb you son of a bitch!" Firing 3 times as fast as I could pull the trigger I shoot 3 Toes in his massive head. Finally, the killer lone wolf named 3 Toes slumped over dead.

After several seconds of watching 3 Toes to make sure he would stay dead, I felt my blood dripping off my right hand. Painfully I took my buckskin shirt off to see if 3 Toes punctured any of the main rivers of blood within my arm. My fear was that 3 Toes had killed me and I just had not bled out yet. With not enough light to see my wounded arm I stumbled with "I want to live" determination and made my way to the fire and with considerable determination pitched 2 more logs on the fire. The dry logs caught quickly, now with a brighter and dancing firelight and I could survey the damage to my arm from the light from the fire. Seeing the puncture wounds to my forearm and although I was in more pain than I could imagine I almost laughed out loud. Thankfully, the thick buckskin shirt had saved my life, although my arm was chewed and looked a mess and would no doubt would take a considerable time to heal I did not believe the puncture wounds had pierced anything vital in my arm. It would seem that luck had been on my side.

Looking now to where Jeb and his unmoving body was I felt the guilt for having fallen asleep and it was now clear that Jeb had tried to take on 3 Toes by himself to protect me. Trying to stand to go check on Jeb I got light-headed and fell back down-hard. Still looking to Jeb I tried to stand again and had made it so I was standing straight up, but my eyesight faltered and I had to close my eyes to keep from passing out. After a few seconds passed, I opened my eyes and they fell upon the unmoving body of my dingo, my partner, my friend Jeb. Trying to move in his direction I slowly took one shaky step and the agonizing pain returned. Along with the pain came the dizziness and I started to fall - this time as I fell - the lights went out.

The wetness on my face revived me some as I slowly opened my eyes. I had been out for quite a spell for the sun was now directly overhead. The sun was out and there was not one cloud in the sky, but my face felt wet. Reaching with my left hand I touched it and it was indeed wet. I started to turn my head to get a better look to see why that was so. It was at this moment when I saw the movement of a cinnamon-colored dingo moving in - to give me another face licking.

Smiling which hurt my face as I sat up slowly and painfully as Jeb just as slow and just as painfully folded into my lap. It would seem that 3 Toes had failed to kill either of us. Looking at my dingo carefully and gingerly I could see he was a chewed upon as I was, but it seemed his wounds like mine were of the healing kind. Holding Jeb's matted and dried bloody head so I could look him in the eye I said, "Jeb, you look like crap my friend. Hell, I guess we both look like crap. Reckon we might just stick to hunting 2 legged critters from here on out."

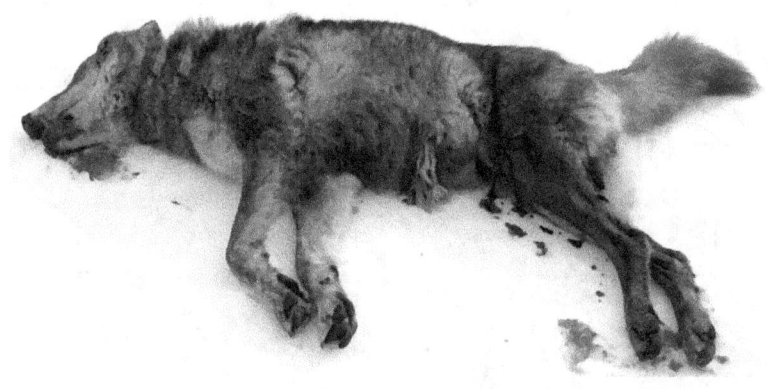

Kurt James

PATTON BOUNTY HUNTER 3RD Adventure

CHAPTER 1

Jeb and I were having a celebration of sorts in the fancy Beaumont Hotel café in Ouray, Colorado. The manager of the establishment was none too happy that I had brought my dingo inside and now had him sitting in one of the elegant dining chairs at the table. After Jeb and I had found an empty table and planted our butts in the chairs, a prim and proper little man with a pencil-thin mustache marched right on over to give us the boot. He stated in a tone more than rude that my "dog" was not welcomed in the Beaumont. Jeb and I just sat there looking at the man without saying one word. The annoying man's face turned red and you could see his frustration building as he was a man used to getting his way and he went on to say, "You must understand, sir, that an establishment of this caliber cannot tolerate having dogs eating from the china. It is uncivilized behavior and not allowed."

Jeb looked at the man then looked at me trying to judge where this conversation was going when I told the little man, "If you are the waiter I reckon we will just have whatever the special is for our supper this evening. One for me and one for my Australian friend."

The proper little fellow gasped so loud you would have thought I had punched him in the gut. He was having a troublesome time trying not to lose his temper and once he finally got control of it again he said. "Sir, my name is Chris Cramer and the owner of this establishment and I must ask you and your dog to leave. If you do not leave, I will have the local law remove you."

Jeb just at that moment decided there was something that needed his attention and the dingo started to lick the top of the ostentatious tablecloth in Mr. Prim and Proper's fancy café. If the owners look had the ability to kill Jeb, and I would have been goners. With a slight chuckle, I told Jeb, "You need to quit licking the table cloth Jeb, Mr. Cramer here has got his knickers all up in a wad."

Jeb stopped licking the table, then just sat there looking at me-wanting me to do something. I was still looking at the Beaumont owner when I said, "Mr. Cramer, Jeb and I have eaten in some of the finest cafes in the Rocky Mountains and I reckon we are going to eat our supper here. The sooner you get us some grub, the sooner we will be on our way." The scrawny and pencil thinned mustache owner stamped his right foot, clicked his heels, and then angrily straightened his vest before stating in a controlled, but angry tone, "What is your name, sir? So, I can tell the Marshal who needs to be removed!"

Still looking at the fuming little man, I pointed at my dingo, "The mutt's name is Jeb, and my name is Dale Lee Patton."

Everyone within the room that was close enough to hear our conversation, including the young Indian boy polishing the brass rail footrest at the bottom of the Beaumont's solid oak bar stopped and waited to see what happened next.

The Beaumont owner face went blank and a bead of sweat broke out on his forehead after hearing my name. The little man's face got all pasty white, and he developed a slight stutter when he next spoke, "Da-Dal-Dale Lee Patton? The bounty hunter gunfighter Dale Lee Patton?"

Nodding my head "yes," before replying to the owner of the Beaumont questions, "Some call me a gunfighter. I really do not care for that handle, because it implies I enjoy the act of shooting people. Sometimes I find it necessary to do so when others take a disliking to Jeb or me. But, I assure you, sir, I shot no one that did not have it coming."

The Beaumont owner now glassy eyes shifted slowly down as if for the first time he saw my brace of two Smith and Wesson Scofield 45's that hung on my hips. His eyes finally rose to look me in the eyes and he finally spoke just above a whisper, "I think the special of the day is a hearty beef stew with freshly baked butter biscuits with a slice of apple pie."

Reaching over to rub Jeb behind his right ear the way he liked it, I said to the owner, "Beef stew and apple pie sounds like the ticket for both Jeb and me. Could you also fetch me a shot of whiskey and 2 glasses of water-one for Jeb and one for me?"

Jeb, my cinnamon-colored dingo, was still sitting in the chair next to me as Mr. Cramer set us both up with our drinks and supper. Jeb was eyeballing the bowl of steaming hot beef stew sitting in front of him and also the one setting in front of me. Jeb kept looking at me, then the bowl of stew - back and forth in anticipation - waiting on me to say it was okay to eat his supper. The dingo from Australia became my bounty-hunting partner several years ago when given to me by an Australian schooner ship captain turned gold prospector on his deathbed. Chuckling to myself for a full minute, I felt sorry for my friend, I finally relented and said, "Remember I get one bowl and you get one bowl. Try not to make a mess of it like the last time we ate in a fancy hotel." Jeb barked once and dug in with all the gusto of a starving mutt. He must have forgotten the part of me saying, "Not to make a mess of it."

We had just collected a $500 bounty of a man named Stan Rogers. Ole' Stan had a dead or alive bounty, a warrant, and was a wanted man in Ouray County for murder and horse theft. Apparently, he had killed a local rancher for the gold in his pocket and the horse he was riding. Once Jeb had caught his scent, we had caught up with the bandit in less than a day. Stan went for his pistol, but was not as handy with it as he thought he was and it forced me to take action and killed the outlaw in a righteous and lawful gunfight.

The young Indian boy that had been polishing the brass rails and spittoons kept staring at Jeb and me as we ate our supper. I finally looked back at him straight in the eye and the youngster's dark brown eyes never wavered. The boy seemed to be possibly 10 or 11 years-old with short black hair. He wore Levi's and a red flannel shirt of the white man, but his Indian heritage and pride was abundant in the way he moved about. If it was my guess, he was Cheyenne or Ute. With our eyes still locked, I said in a pleasant tone, "If you got something to say son, spit it out."

The boy was silent for a few seconds as he was gathering his thoughts; I waved him over closer to me. The boy did not hesitate and made his way until he was standing next to Jeb's chair and was looking at me. Jeb stood up on the armrest of his chair with his tail spinning so rapidly that any fly that would have been in its path would have met its death because of tail wagging. Jeb leaned forward enough to lay his head on the young Indian's left shoulder, which told me everything I needed to know about the boy. As soon as Jeb touched the youngster, the boy's face lit up with an enormous smile and he reached with his right hand to scratch Jeb behind his ears just as if he instinctively knew that was the dingo's favorite spot. If Jeb liked the kid, then the boy had a good heart. I trusted Jeb's instincts towards people more than my own.

Looking the boy in the eye and I knew what was inside this boy was clever, but troubled. Smiling, I said, "Son, what is your name?"

The Indian boy answered without hesitation, "Minninnewah, is my name."

Running his name through my thinker, I realized it was Cheyenne, but I could not interpret the meaning into English, "What does your name mean in the white man's language?"

Again, without hesitation, he said, "It means Wild Wind, but the man that owns me calls me Reggie."

The hair on my arm tingled when I heard the boy tell me another owned him. I did not cotton to that idea at all. I would have to ponder on that for a spell, so as I ran that around in my brainpan for a few minutes I said, "Wild Wind is a strong Cheyenne name and it is fitting for one such as yourself - so I shall call you by your given name Wild Wind."

To the delight of Jeb - Wild Wind was still scratching the dingo's ears. I could feel the loneliness of the boy as he stood there giving my dingo the pleasure of his company. My mother was a Ute Indian, and I understood this boy more than he could ever know. The boy looked as if he was holding back saying what he wanted to tell me, so I said, "Wild Wind my name is Dale Patton, and since we are now friends, you can say what you want to say to me. You need to understand what we share with a friend is just for the two of us and no one else needs to know. So, if you got something you want to say-spit it out."

Wild Wind smile disappeared as he thought about what he was going to say. Finally, he had gathered his thoughts and said to me, "Mr. Patton, I have heard of you and I know your job is finding people. I want to hire you to find my mother!"

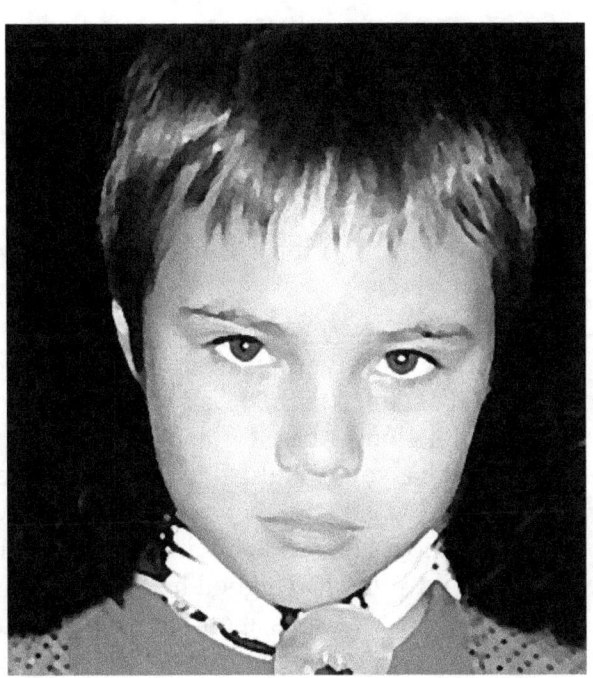

CHAPTER 2

At that moment, I could almost feel the callow boy's pain. His dark eyes reflected the misery of his heart. So many times a youngster will be abandoned in the Rocky Mountains by mothers and fathers that can no longer care for them. I had no respect for those that might leave a young child at the mercy of one's like Chris Cramer. If Wild Wind's mother sold him into slavery, then he was better off without her. Jeb knew it right off from the start and I now felt it. Wild Wind had a good heart and deserved a better start in life than this. Now curious about the young Indian boy, I wanted to hear his story. Pointing at a third seat empty at the table, I said in a matter-of-fact voice, "Sit down Wild Wind so we can open up a negotiation."

Wild Wind became nervous and rocked back and forth on the balls of his feet as he looked around the room for the man that owned him. Knowing he felt he would be in trouble, I tried to ease his mind and I said in a clear and forceful voice, "If the owner of this establishment has an issue of you sitting and talking to me; he will have to take that issue up with me. So, please Wild Wind by all means sit down so we can talk."

A smile split the young boy's face, and he quickly took the seat. Jeb decided at that moment to leave his chair and joined Wild Wind in his. The dingo cuddled up next to the youngster and lay half of his body in Wild Wind's lap. It would seem that Jeb and Wild Wind had become fast friends. Seeing both Jeb and the boy settled in, I asked Wild Wind, "You said you wanted to hire me. What were you thinking in the form of payment for my services?"

Wild Wind looked around the room as if he didn't want anyone to look at him at this moment and he slowly produced a $5 gold piece from his pocket as he spoke, "I found this last night on the floor when I was cleaning. I asked the men standing at the bar at the time if it had been theirs and they all said it was 'finder's keepers' so I kept it, then hid it from Mr. Cramer. Mr. Patton I know it is not much, but it is all I have."

My chest felt tight at that very moment, because I knew in my gut that the boy to be truthful. Reaching out, I took the gold piece and felt the weight of it, then I laid it on top of the table in between Wild Wind and myself. Wild Wind had nothing when he found the $5 and tried to find the owner of the gold piece. To him that $5 had to be a fortune, and he was willing to give it all to me as payment. As a bounty hunter, I had been paid in impressive sums of money and gold to locate people, but I had never been paid with everything that a person owned. If possible, I had decided that Jeb and I would help this Cheyenne boy. There was one thing I needed to clear up before asking him about his mother, "Wild Wind, do you know where your father is?"

Wild Wind nodded his head "yes," before speaking in a subdued voice, "My father was killed when I was 6 years-old by Mexican bandits. My mother and I became slaves when the same bandits captured us sold us to the Comancheros down south. When I was eight, they sold my mother and me to a mountain man named Reno that brought us back up north here to Colorado to set his traps and skin his hides. My mother fought Reno several times with a knife and wounded him severely once. Reno sold the 2 of us to Mr. Cramer 3 months ago, because he feared my mother would kill him."

Even though slavery was one of the reasons they had fought the Civil War for and Ole' Abe Lincoln had it abolished. The misery of servitude and bondage still raised its ugly head from time to time, even on the Rocky Mountain frontier, especially with the Indian tribes. This callow Cheyenne lad deserved a better chance at life than what fate had dealt him so far, and Jeb and I would do what we could do to make that happen. With a heavy heart I asked Wild Wind, "Tell me about your mother."

Wild Wind eyes wetted as he spoke, "My mother... She is beautiful, softened, but she can be hard and brave. When it is just the two of us she smiles a lot. And I always wondered if my smile was as big as hers. Maybe as big I think, but not as beautiful. At night she holds me and sings songs of our ancestors until I fall asleep. Sometimes in the quiet moments I want to crawl inside her mind to find that place that lets her smile and sing through the misery and the beatings. Reno and Mr. Cramer called her crazy because she would fight them. If I had to be crazy, I want to be my mama's kind of crazy, because she is never afraid."

Wild Wind's heartfelt passage made me think of my wife and the misery she had gone through when she had been brutally murdered. The love Wild Wind felt for his mother brought a tear to my eye and made my heart sing. Jeb the dingo felt it, and he pulled in closer to the young boy to comfort him. Reaching out I gently laid my hand on Wild Wind's right shoulder and looked him straight in the eye and said in a voice full of conviction, "Jeb and I will move heaven and the earth to find your mother. You just hired the best bounty hunter duo in the Rocky Mountains. What is your mother's name and when was the last time you saw her?"

Wild Wind slid the $5 gold piece across the table closer to me as he spoke in a broken voice, "My mother's name is Wynoka, and 2 men came into our shack we lived in behind the Beaumont 2 weeks ago while we were sleeping and gagged my mother's mouth and tied her feet and hands and dragged her off. She fought and spit on the men, but they were too strong. Mr. Cramer held the door as they took her out. Once the men had left through the door Mr. Cramer locked me in. A minute later I could hear the horses and the creak of a buggy seat as they took her away. I have not seen or heard of her since."

The name Wynoka was Cheyenne, and this I knew translated to English meant Sweet Water. They had kidnapped Sweet Water in the middle of the night in front of her son as if he was not even there. And the owner of this establishment stood by and watched. I was seething inside, and my anger was on the rise. I had learned in my life where there was anger, there was pain beneath it. I had to take control of that anger and the pain and use it as a tool. One thing was for certain and that was Wild Wind would not spend another day of his life in the servitude of Chris Cramer. Just as that last thought rambled through my mind Cramer walked into the dining room and saw Wild Wind sitting at my table.

Cramer, by the ole' stink eye that the prim and proper little man with the pencil-thin mustache was shooting my way - he was sullen as a sore-headed dog. I knew Cramer being the skunk he was would never try to brace me on his own, but it seemed he had recruited a pair of hard-cases.

Pushing the $5 gold piece back across the table to Wild Wind, I said, "No need for payment yet. First, I have to find your mother."

Cramer, feeling brave now that he had other gents to handle the rough stuff, marched in our tables' direction. And in a loud and demanding voice said, "Reggie, back to work! Mr. Patton, you have overstayed your welcome in the Beaumont. You and the gnarly beast need to leave or I will have you thrown out!"

CHAPTER 3

Wild Wind stiffened when Cramer called him by his slave name and told him to get back to work. I winked at him and pointed at the $5 gold piece before speaking, "Son, pocket your money, you don't pay until I find your mother."

Slowly I stood to my full height of 6'2" as I turned to face Cramer and his hired guns. My 200 pounds was a tad larger than either of the 2 soldier of fortune wannabes standing in front of me. Talking in a loud and clear voice so there was no misunderstanding, "Glad you are here Mr. Cramer, saves me the trouble of tracking you down. The boy you call Reggie is named Wild Wind, and he is a proud member of the Cheyenne tribe and you will address him as such!"

Cramer face turned red as his fury flared and he was feeling his oats since he had two rough compadres to back his play. Both men stood off to the left, and I recognized neither of them. They both wore one Colt pistol in a holster strapped on their right legs. Both men were dressed similar with dark Stetsons, Levi's, and button down flannel shirts. The only actual difference was the one on the right was a good 4 inches taller. They had the traits, and the look of dusty cowboys that worked the trail herds. Both were built lean, and I knew that they probably were excellent cowhands. Their pistols were clean and well taken care of and I could only assume that they had been offered money to make me leave the Beaumont. What the 2 hired guns did not know was - nobody makes Dale Lee Patton leave - nobody. If it was a gunfight they wanted I would accommodate them. Cramer was not armed - so at the moment he was no threat. Cramer was still thinking he had the upper hand, and he almost shouted, "I will call the boy anything I want - since I ow…" Cramer stopped himself from revealing the true-type of man he was in a dining room full of witnesses.

Smiling, I said, "Finish what you were saying Mr. Cramer 'since I own the heathen'. Just so you know Wild Wind will leave with me and there is nothing you are these 2 gents can do about it. I cotton little to men that hold themselves in high regards to others and hires two bums to do his dirty work."

The taller gunman's eyes tapered and gave him away as he started to draw. He never cleared leather before I fast palmed both of my Smith and Wesson Scofield 45's with a speed that neither of the cowhands had seen before. I pointed one of my weapons at each gun hand. I didn't fire and both of the mercenaries knew I held their lives in my pistols. Silence overwhelmed the room and the second hand of the clock behind the bar sounded like a beating drum. Slowly both cowboys raised their hands away from their weapons, hoping that they may see the next minute of the day. Looking at the taller wannabe dangerous man in the eyes, "It seems your boys luck is running a bit muddy. You may take your leave and I mean leave. You best be nimble-footed and on your horses and on the way out of town before I hit the boardwalk in front of this hotel. If I ever see you again, I will kill you. Now, scat!"

Both of the hired guns about fell twice, tripping over chairs on their way out. They didn't look back even once as they banged through the batwing doors. Looking at Wild Wind, his mouth was wide open, and he looked as if he was in shock. Jeb on the other hand had fallen asleep in Wild Winds lap - so much for back-up from the dingo. Holstering my left-handed Scofield - I then pointed the right-handed pistol at Cramer's head as I moved within arm's length of the Beaumont owner.

Cramer bowed his head and could not look me in the eye as his bottom lip quivered. In a broken voice that sounded like a baby whimper Cramer pleaded with me, "Don't kill me Mr. Patton. I have money I can give you!"

Waiting a full minute, letting Cramer soil his long johns before I spoke, "You are unarmed, so I will not kill you, but I am sure as hell going to beat the shit out of you!"

Cramer raised his head and his eyes widen as he finally met my gaze. Once he was looking down the barrel of my pistol, I flipped it in a practice maneuver so now I was gripping the barrel of the Scofield. Almost in the same motion as flipping my weapon, I brought the butt of the grip down hard on Cramer's head for a classic pistol whipping.

Head wounds bleed something fierce and Cramer's fresh noggin wound was no different as he dropped to the floor like a 160 pound bag of potatoes. Holstering my Scofield, I stood over Cramer laying in his own blood on the floor of the establishment he owned. I rolled him over with my right foot and was a little disgusted when Mr. Prim and Proper's blood stained my boot. Once Cramer was on his back, I reached down and savagely picked him up by grabbing his very expensive and shiny button down vest. Then I placed him not so gently into a vacant chair at our table.

Cramer was still dumbfounded as I unsheathed my 12 inch Bowie knife as I pulled up a chair next to his chair. Sitting down, I stabbed the Bowie knife into the top of the table so it was within the reach of both Cramer and myself. Waiting for almost a full minute for Cramer's noodle to clear. Once I saw his eyes clear a tad from being glazed over and thought he could comprehend what I was about to say. Pointing at the Bowie I spoke in a casual tone as if we had been friends since childhood, "See the Bowie knife, if at any time you don't like how this negotiation is going and you want to end it you can make a grab for the knife. And we will then settle this in a more of a Rocky Mountain frontier style. Do you understand?"

Cramer's bottom lip still quivered as he drooled his answer, "Yes sir, Mr. Patton. There will be no need for the Bowie knife. Although I don't understand, what negotiation?"

Letting Cramer sweat for a spell I looked at Wild Wind who was still sitting in his chair in disbelief as Jeb was still asleep in his lap and starting to snore. Still looking at Wild Wind I pointed at my Australian trail partner and in a pleasant matter-of-fact voice said, "Jeb falls asleep like that after he grubs and gets a full belly.

Wild Wind was a little dumbfounded on what was going on, but when I spoke of Jeb, he looked at my dingo and then looked at me and a half-smile formed. I was sure he had never seen his boss being manhandled like I was doing and did not have a clue where this confrontation was going.

Now turning back my full attention to Chris Cramer and I spoke in a commanding voice, "Yes, a negotiation. I will ask you some questions and you will answer them truthfully and when I am satisfied with your answers, you are going to give me a few things and Wild Wind, Jeb, and I will take our leave. If I feel you are lying to me or fail to give me what I want, I will beat the shit out of you again. I am not even pissed you hired a couple of slow on the draw dimwits to throw me out or shoot me down. However, what makes me mad as a bear with 2 cubs and a sore teat is when you decided to purchase and enslave Wild Wind and his mother. Once you slapped down the cash or gold to purchase a human being, you agreed to the terms of this negotiation. Do you savvy, Mr. Cramer?"

Cramer's tears flowed freely and his body twitched, and the stench of him soiling his long johns again filled the air. A half-minute passed by before the owner of the Beaumont could get himself under control before he spoke almost in a whisper, "I understand Mr. Patton."

Leaning closer to Cramer to intimidate him even more I asked, "Now that we understand each other Mr. Cramer, where is Wild Wind's mother Sweet Water?"

Cramer's head sunk even lower as he didn't want to answer my question, but I knew he would and he would tell me the truth. He wanted me gone and to never, ever see me again. Giving him a little time to collect his thoughts and himself, I sat back in my chair and waited. Cramer finally cleared his throat and mumbled, "The boy's mother is at the mining camp of Copper Glen at the base of the Red Mountains."

Sitting back, I reflected on what the owner of the Beaumont had just told me. Red Mountains is a set of 3 peaks in the San Juan Mountains. The 3 mountains get their name from the reddish iron ore rocks that covers the surface, but the splendid news of the day is that mining camp of Copper Glen was only 5 or 6 miles south of Ouray. Leaning forward once again, I asked, "Copper Glen is sprawled out over a sizeable area. Where exactly will I locate Sweet Water?"

Cramer lowered his chin even further and closed his eyes before he answered, "She will be at the Watershed."

I wanted to kill Cramer right then. Taking control of the rage that was building within me I said in a disgusted voice, "So, let's see if I got this right you separated a mother and a son from each other when you 'sold' her into prostitution! Is that about right?"

Cramer slowly nodded his head "yes," then he tried to justify his actions when in a rush to explain himself said, "I didn't want to separate the two, but the mother was a handful and fought me several times and tried to stab me with a fork. I was afraid she would kill me some night in my sleep. I had to get rid of her."

Of course Sweet Water wanted to kill him, who would not have wanted to kill this puny little man in that situation. Sitting back again to reflect on this last tidbit of news, I realized rescuing Sweet Water had now become an almost impossible task. The brothel named Watershed at Copper Glen was owned and operated by the well-known gunfighter named Morgan Dean.

CHAPTER 4

Before Wild Wind, Jeb, and I walked out of the Beaumont Hotel I had Chris Cramer give me a bill of sale for 2 of his horses and 2 saddles that he had owned. It was he did that or I would have pistol whipped him until he did. Mr. Cramer decided that one head wound was enough for the day and gladly signed over the bill of sale for the 4-year-old horses and saddles. Cramer told us where we could pick-up the horses. Both of Wild Wind and Sweet Water new horses and saddles were stabled at the same livery stable that Cinders my blood bay three-year-old mare was at.

Before stepping out onto the boardwalk of the Beaumont, I sent Jeb out first. It was a possibility that the gents Cramer had hired to beat or shoot me down could be waiting in ambush. Watching the dingo through the batwing doors he seemed to take his leisure sitting on the boardwalk watching the comings and goings of the late day, early night activity of Ouray. After a full minute I finally chuckled and said to furry friend, "Jeb, are you doing your job checking for a trap or are you just lollygagging?"

Jeb turned his head and looked over his shoulder back at me with his jackass eating cactus grin. It was so comical even Wild

Wind laughed. Looking at Wild Wind with a smile, "Must be safe since Jeb is not fussing around and still sitting on his end gate."

As Wild Wind and I stepped out onto the boardwalk, we witness the very thing that made me know I was living in the most stunning place in the world. The sun was just finishing its round for the day and was starting to slowly sink below the snowcapped peaks in the west. The orange and blue hue of a Rocky Mountain sunset never ceased to amaze me. Speaking to Wild Wind like we were at this moment the only 2 people in the world, "Folks, especially townsfolk nowadays, don't take the time to watch the sunset like they should. They take for granted they will see another one the next day. Life is tough in these mountains and death is just one hardship away and it does not guarantee your next day. So remember Wild Wind, whatever you are doing take a moment and treat yourself to the beauty of a mountain sunset each and every day."

It would seem that Cramer although lacking any caring for his fellow man had an eye for horses. The horses previously owned by the Beaumont Hotel owner and now owned by Wild Wind and his mother Sweet Water were of excellent stock. Both horses were almost identical Chestnuts and stood at 16 hands. The only difference was that the one named Ginger had a white stocking on her right front foreleg where the horse named Flame was all chestnut color.

After getting all the horses saddle, I thought it was best that we leave Ouray as quickly as possible. A man like Cramer had more money than brains and may try to recruit others to plant me into a shallow grave.

Copper Glen mining camp at the base of the Red Mountains was less than a 1½ hour ride. Enough time to reflect on what I knew about the gunfighter Morgan Dean, the owner of the brothel named Watershed.

Wild Wind was riding his new mare Ginger while Flame's reins were tethered to the saddle on his horse. The youngster was now quiet and lost in his own thoughts. I am sure when the young Cheyenne woke up this morning he could not have even imagined how the events of the day would turn out. Hell, there was no way I could have imagined it. A day of rest after a successful bounty was what I had in mind. And here I was riding into the night with Wild

Wind to find his mother. The only thing I had to do was convince one of the most feared gunmen on the Rocky Mountain frontier was to let her go. One way or another, the end of this adventure would be at the Watershed in Copper Glen.

The cinnamon-colored short-haired Jeb as always had taken point and he would race ahead on the trail for a 100 feet and then sit and wait for us to catch up. When Jeb the dingo had been given to me by a dying Australian ship Captain turned gold miner I worried if he could adapt to the high altitude and the cold of the high country. Jeb didn't just adapt to this country, he became part of the mountains. It was as if he had been mountain bred all along. I loved that pain in the butt dingo something fierce.

Looking at the proud adolescent man riding next to me as we rode in silence that in many ways Wild Wind reminded me of myself. My mother Walk With Ghost and my step-father, the legendary mountain man Matt Lee, taught me to never back down or be ashamed of where I came from. I have known Wild Wind for less than a day and I could see he carried his Cheyenne Indian heritage well. It would seem even though Sweet Water and Wild Wind had been in a no-win situation since the boy's father had been killed. It was encouraging to me that the youngster's mother could still teach her son to be proud of who he was. I had committed myself to right a wrong inflicted on this boy and his mother, and there was nothing short of death that could prevent me from fulfilling my promise to find Wild Wind's mother and reunite them—nothing!

The night had cooled and the night breeze out of the north felt soothing on my face as it gently caressed it. The smell of early autumn rode the wind as the decay of the aspen leaves was just starting. After the death of autumn then the bone-chilling cold and silence of a high mountain winter would savagely roll across the timberline. The autumn and the winter months in the high country spoke to the half Ute Indian and half mountain man that I was.

As the night wore on, a half-moon lit up the cloudless sky overhead as I remembered all the stories I had heard about Morgan Dean. By all accounts Dean was a sporting man who had won and lost many of a fortune by "bucking the tiger" playing Faro. Almost all of his 7 or 8 gunfights had come about over disagreements over the poker or Faro table. Although I had never seen the man his reputation with his Colt pistol was fast becoming legendary on par with the likes of Bill Hickok, Lance Eldridge, Chance Bondurant, and the man that raised me Matt Lee. I had heard about 6 months ago that Dean had gained ownership of the brothel named the Watershed in Copper Glen for payment over a gambling debt. I did not care one way or another if the man was a gambler, brothel owner, or deadly accurate when defending himself. What I could not abide was the fact he had purchased Sweet Water and was forcing her into prostitution.

It wasn't long before we had reached the northern end of Copper Glen. The smell of cook fires and burnt meat filled the air as everyone here was just finishing up their supper. I had been in Copper Glen once before and to the best of my knowledge the mining settlement did not have a sheriff. The only law that existed in places like this was the law of the fittest or the fastest. The Watershed brothel was in the center of the settlement on a well-traveled and rutted dirt road that served as the major street of this boom town.

Most of Copper Glen was tents and shacks. There were only 2 wood framed buildings in the entire town. The Watershed was one and across the street was the other one, an eatery and saloon called the Mountain Apple. The only hitching rail in the whole settlement was in front of the Mountain Apple, which I headed for first.

Once in front of the hitching post, I saw the orange and reddish glow of burning tobacco from someone in the shadows taking a pull on their evening pipe. Still keeping an eye on the man in the shadows I dismounted then the man spoke, and it was a voice I knew, "Well if it is not the famous bounty hunter Dale Lee Patton and his trusted dog Jeb from down under. Is this lad some offspring of yours or someone you are collecting a bounty on?"

Smiling now as I tied off Cinder to the hitching post, I looked at Wild Wind then pointed to the hitching post so he would know to tie off Ginger and Flame. As Wild Wind went about his chore, I turned to the man in the shadows and laughingly said, "Wild Wind is neither a bounty nor an offspring. Sitting in the shadows is an excellent way to startle someone and get yourself shot. Copper Glen is a tad off your range, Mr. Ford. What are you doing here on this fine evening?"

Russell Ford, the gray-haired aging owner of the Ford Gulch cattle ranch Near Breckenridge, stood and stepped forward out of the shadows so I could see him in the moonlight. Recently Jeb and I tracked down a killer wolf named 3 Toes for a $1000 bounty paid by another cattle rancher named Vincent Moore. Jeb and I had gotten to know Mr. Ford from picking up the elusive wolf's scent on his ranch after 3 Toes had slaughter some Ford Gulch ranch yearling's cows. Mr. Ford was kind enough to supply grub and supplies for Jeb and I for the duration of our hunt for the wolf. That wolf bounty almost ended up being the death of both Jeb and myself, and Mr. Ford let us heal up from the war wounds of our battle with 3 Toes on his ranch for a week. In that brief time that Mr. Ford and I had known each other, we had become friends. Mr. Ford took another pull on his pipe and replied, "Two of my hands and I trailed some cows over from my range on the Blue River. These rock hounds here in Copper Glenn got to eat and we are supplying them with beefsteaks."

Ford was still wanting to shoot the gab said, "Dale, what brings you this far south?"

Pulling my right-handed Scofield and then my left-handed one checking to make sure I was fully loaded as I continued to talk to Mr. Ford, "Looking for this boy's mother and I have reason to believe she is in the Watershed across the street."

That got Mr. Ford's attention, and he stood a little straighter when he spoke, "The Watershed? The cathouse? Does she work there?"

Nodding my head "yes," I also replied, "She does, but not willingly and I am going to fetch her and reunite her with her son."

Mr. Ford face showed surprise and in an almost stutter said, "Dale do you know who owns the Watershed?"

Once I was satisfied my Smith and Wesson's Scofield's were fully loaded I slid them easily into the holsters on each side. Taking a deep breath, I answered, "I do Mr. Ford, and I reckon I will not find Morgan Dean sitting on his gun hand when I take this boy's mom out of there!"

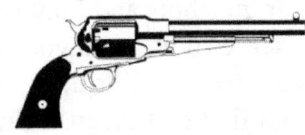

CHAPTER 5

Still standing at the hitching rail in front of the Mountain Apple I spoke to Wild Wind, "Now this is where the going gets tough in getting your mother. I need you to walk into the Watershed with me since I do not know what your mother looks like. Once she sees you I need you to hustle her out there like a cat with his tail afire. Get her across the street and both of you get saddled up on Ginger and Flame. Here are the bill of sales for the 2 horses and saddles in case anyone questions you about them. I had Cramer sign them over to you. Here is another envelope that you need to hold on to for me, but you can't open it unless I don't make it out. This is important Wild Wind - once you have your mother don't look back or come back in the Watershed. Not going to lie or sugarcoat it son, there probably will be gunplay and people may die, might even be me. If you hear gunshots and I am the first one out the door after the gunfire settles down and your mother and you are in the saddle, wait for me, and we will ride out of here together. If someone else comes out first that means I didn't make it and you take the horses and you get your mother out of Copper Glen as fast as you can. If I don't make it, but Jeb does when you hightail it out of here - call to him and he will go with you. Do you understand?"

Wild Wind took the envelope and the 2 bill of sales and stuffed them in his Levi pocket on his hip. This young Cheyenne boy was all that I thought he was when I first laid eyes on him. He was a little nervous with what was about to happen, but he showed no fear. He would be a hell of a man someday. What ever happened here today I was proud to be associated with reuniting this boy and his mother. I knew my wife if she were still alive would have been just as proud. Wild Wind answered me is a strong and commanding voice, "I understand Mr. Patton."

Jeb knew from experiences with me that we both knew the cards had been dealt and it was time to let destiny decide our fate. It was at times like this that Jeb always became as calm as a toad in the sun in front of a gathering storm. I was ready, and so was Jeb.

Russell Ford being the principled man that he was said matter-of-factly from the boardwalk, "Dale if you need a couple of extra guns I will get my boys and we will go with you to get the boy's mother."

Turning I looked at my friend Russell and replied, "Thoughtful of you Russell, but I am the one picking this fight, and I need to finish it."

Having said that with Wild Wind on my right side and Jeb on my left side, we started walking across the rutted road to the front steps of the Watershed. There we climbed the 3 wooden steps before reaching the flat of the boardwalk and the batwing doors of the Watershed. Taking a deep breath, we pushed through and walked in.

It would seem that Morgan Dean's cathouse was a thriving business with 5 soiled doves making the rounds strolling in front of 7 men enticing them with their charms. A 6th woman sat off in the corner and by the look of her she was a full blood Indian woman. A very striking and beautiful woman. She was small in frame with long black hair that was braided and was hung over her shoulder much like you would see in a painting hanging in some museum somewhere. Her dark brown eyes showed only misery of one that possibly that had lost all hope. She looked like Wild Wind, and I knew the woman in the corner was the boy's mother, Sweet Water.

There was a small bar in the room, and 2 men sat at it. Both men were sizeable and looked to be kin of some sort. Both men were over 6 feet tall and in their early fifties with short salt and pepper hair. Each man by themselves outweighed me by about 50 pounds. They both were armed with Colts in their tied down holsters on their right legs. I wondered if one of them was the notorious Morgan Dean.

Sweet Water eyes searched the room, and as she did so they finally fell upon her son. At first her eyes showed no recognition. Then finally it sunk in that her son was here in the room with her and then her eyes widen in disbelief. I watched her for a few seconds as she sat there as if she was dumbfounded. When it all became clear in her mind she jumped up and rushed across the room and gathered her son up in her arms and held him tight. As soon as she had moved swiftly through the room it caught the attention of one of the big men sitting at the bar and he spun around and in a loud an angry voice, "Squaw, what the hell are you doing?"

Wild Wind looked to me for direction when I told him in a loud and clear voice, "Get your mother out of here and do what I said earlier."

Sweet Water looked confused as her eyes caught mine as she was trying to put together why her son was here and why I was with him. Wild Wind took control of the situation liked I hoped he would and he started moving his mother gently out the batwing doors. Sweet Water reached out and touched my arm as if she needed to feel that I was real and not a dream.

The sizeable man that spoke earlier almost yelled, "Wait one minute, stranger! Who are you to be running off with my help? Do you know who I am?"

The hackles on Jeb's back stood straight up, and he snarled at the loud talker. Jeb was ready and Jeb was willing for whatever came next.

The tension in the air was almost like a lightning bolt had flashed in the Watershed and all the scarlet ladies and all the men in the room could feel it. Everyone in the room did not understand what to do as their eyes went back and forth from the loud talker and me. Waiting to answer the question for a few seconds until I was sure that Sweet Water and Wild Wind had gained their saddles on Ginger and Flame. In a clear voice, "I reckon you are Morgan Dean, the owner of this establishment. The woman you just called 'squaw' is named Sweet Water, and she is not here willingly. You bought her from a man named Chris Cramer in Ouray, and I have come to fetch her to reunite her with her son. If it is money you want, I will pay you what you paid for her or I will take her by force if needed. Either way, she is leaving with me. Your call Mr. Dean."

Well, I might as well have yelled fire—for everyone except the two men at the bar didn't piddle around and moved silently, but quickly to the batwing doors and the outside. Jeb and I both stepped to my right about 6 feet so all the fair belles and now frustrated cowpokes could make a hasty retreat. With the Watershed now empty except for Jeb and the 3 of us, it would seem the 3rd unknown man would back Morgan Dean's play. The 3rd man stood and stood next to Morgan and spread his feet under his shoulders in the classic gunfighter stance. Morgan was looking at me in skepticism as he chuckled slightly and without taking his eyes off of me he said to the man standing next to him, "Do you believe this shit Dutch? This gun-slick comes in my place and takes what is mine. Hard to believe!"

It all made sense now. I had heard that Dutch Adams and Morgan Dean were related, 1st cousins, was the rumor I heard. Looking at them standing side by side there was no doubt they were kin, they almost looked like brothers. Dutch Adams was suspected in several stage and bank robberies in and around Durango, Colorado, but never proven. He also had the reputation as a gun-hand like his cousin. The prospect of facing 2 men with these types of reputations did nothing to alter what I had come here to do. My mind already focused on what was to come with all of my sense's being alert and ready. I could see every droplet of sweat on both man's faces, I could hear the people milling about outside trying to be quiet by whispering to each other waiting for an outcome. I could smell the stink of the outhouse out back. My killer instinct was ready. Jeb was ready.

Dutch Adams looked a tad confused and asked, "Who are you?"

My eyes narrowed as I answered—they deserved to know who would kill them today, "My name is Dale Lee Patton!"

They were not expecting that. Now they knew the man they faced, and the worry flashed across their faces, for they knew of me and my abilities. This confrontation had already gone too far for men of our stature to withdraw, they both knew it, and I knew it. Dutch Adams' eyes gave him away as he started his draw, he reached, he fumbled, and that was his fatal mistake.

Jeb started his attack for Morgan Dean when I palmed both of my Smith & Wesson's with practice lightning speed. Dutch Adams never cleared his holster as I placed 2 shots just above his belt buckle and the killing shot in his forehead as he fell. Jeb's attack startled Morgan Dean like he had forgotten about the dingo standing at my feet. Jeb probably saved my life for Morgan Dean's reputation as a fast draw was accurate. He had been faster than me, but had been thrown off by Jeb's attack and Morgan Dean's first and only shot missed. The whine of the bullet passing my head is a hint in any man's language as I fired. My first shot took Morgan in the belt buckle, as I walked them up as the second bullet took him in the middle of his chest and the 3rd bullet punched in and out of his throat. Both cousins were dead before they hit the floor.

CHAPTER 6

Jeb in the aftermath of the shoot-out gently sniffed the bodies of the 2 men now as their life blood creeped slowly across the wooden floor. Looking at Morgan Dean and his cousin Dutch Adams lying dead on the floor, because I took their lives. Everything they had been or would have been had been snuffed out, because one of them did not see the wrong of enslaving someone. The world was not perfect and most times the solution to a problem has end-of-life consequences. This was one of those times. There is beauty in life, and then there is the finality of death. What I have done cannot be undone and I have to live with that. Death was something I could see, understand, and try to learn from it. What I could not do was feel guilty, fearful or remorseful for the events on this day. I had to gain wisdom for what had happened.

Walking out onto the boardwalk in front of the Watershed, the rutted road in front of me was filled with Copper Glens residents. The aftermath of a shoot-out in any mining camp or town along the

Rocky Mountain frontier was the spectacle of the day, and tomorrow there would be 100 unique versions of what happened. I could see Sweet Water and Wild Wind sitting on their horses and their faces showed the relief and happiness of the outcome of the shoot-out. Their smiles made everything that had happened today worthwhile. Stepping off the boardwalk, Jeb and I made our way through the crowd and the questions towards them.

Even before I got to the other side of the road, Wild Wind and Sweet Water quickly dismounted. Wild Wind and his mother both fell into my arms as if we were family and had known each other forever. It made my heart sing to bring these two back together. Jeb was at our feet spinning, prancing, and barking like a new pup. As we all were standing there Russell Ford appeared by my side after he had gone inside the Watershed and viewed the aftermath of what happened. He touched my arm and said, "I have never been impressed much by others and their brag. Dale, you are no bragger, you are a man of integrity with the means to stop those that prey upon others. Dutch Adams and Morgan Dean were men that preyed upon the weak and helpless. I am impressed. I got to ask Dale, what's next for you? What is next for Sweet Water and Wild Wind?"

Looking at my friend I was confused, and I was sure my face showed it. I had been so focused on finding Sweet Water I had not thought about what was next once that mission was completed. Did I just save Sweet Water and Wild Wind from the injustice of being enslaved only to let them become victims again to those that prey on the weak?

Still holding Sweet Water and Wild Wind tight, I answered Mr. Ford, "I reckon I am not sure what is next. They are free to make their own way now, but I fear they will be future victims until Wild Wind becomes of age."

Russell moved in closer and he said with a smile as he spoke directly to Sweet Water and Wild Wind, "Dale, I may have a workable solution. I would like to offer both Sweet Water and Wild Wind jobs at my ranch. I have a small cabin separated away from the principal house and they can live there and work there as long as they want. That way when you are in Blue River country you can stop by and visit more often."

Tears flowed from mother and son as they both nodded their heads "yes". What a grand gesture by an honorable man to offer them a place to work and live where I knew they would be safe. This was a day to remember for sure. Bending down to get eye level with Wild Wind, I reached out and gently wiped a tear from his face when I said, "Wild Wind time to finish our deal."

Wild Wind's face lit up with a jack-o'-lantern grin as he reached in his pocket and produced what was there and handed over to me the contents, "Yes, we do, Mr. Patton. A deal is a deal."
Wild Wind produced the bill of sale for Ginger and Flame and the saddles, the white envelope I had given him, and the $5 gold piece. The bill of sale I handed back to him. The white envelope had $500 in cash which was the bounty money Jeb and I had earned for Stan Rogers - I handed that envelope to Sweet Water. The $5 gold piece I held it so Wild Wind would get his last look at it before I dropped it into my vest pocket. Grinning I said, "Wild Wind, that $5 gold piece was for the bounty of finding your mother and you are now paid in full. The horses and saddles are yours, courtesy of Mr. Cramer. Sweet Water that envelope is yours to keep, just promise me you will not open it until tomorrow after I am long gone on the trail. I am sure you will find a use for it."

Kurt James

PATTON
BOUNTY
HUNTER
4th
Adventure

CHAPTER 1

Jeb, the cinnamon-colored short-haired Australian born dingo, Cinders my blood bay three-year-old mare, and I held up on a ridge overlooking the railroad camp of Cimarron, Colorado. Using my binoculars I surveyed the camp below me looking for anything out of the ordinary, like if a sheriff's office had sprung up since the last time I was here 6 months ago. Jeb and I were currently unemployed, and I was hoping to thumb through some wanted posters. Being a bounty hunter, you were only as wealthy as the next bounty. Seeing one new wood framed building that was not there before; I gave Cinders some rein and her head and we moved out slowly towards Cimarron.

Sweat was pouring off my face as the day had grown warm. The scorching August sun was directly overhead without a cloud in sight. The green leaves of the aspens trees were silent, for there was no breeze to orchestrate them into their song of the quaking. The only sound was the creak of my saddle and the "clang" of a blacksmith hammer in the distance.

The Denver and Rio Grande railroad had just months before completed the railroad track through the Black Canyon and at the end of the canyon the railroad camp we were riding into had sprung up. Some say that this railroad would be the primary source of transportation of shipping valuable ore that had been mined throughout the San Juan Mountains.

Cimarron was more of a tent camp than a town. The ruts in the major road going into the camp would have presented difficult footing for Cinders, so we blazed a fresh trail along the old trail. Jeb had taken point, I believed the mutt was excited for the sights and sounds of the encampment. Me, not so much, I preferred the solitude of the Rocky Mountains. Not that I was not a civilized man; it was because in my profession I dealt with mostly the hard cases, half-wits, killers, rapists, and murders that roamed the timberline of these mountains I called home.

The wood-framed building to my disappointment was not a sheriff's office, so there would be no wanted posters to look at. Although, the poorly framed one-story building called the Elk Saloon had an eatery for grub you didn't have to trap, kill, clean, or fry yourself. Pulling back slightly on Cinders reins in front of the Elk Saloon, I waited until Jeb was done peeing on everything and everyone that stood still long enough for him to pee on. There was more than a few stink eyes from folks that Jeb had marked with his scent, but all had noticed my brace of 2 Smith & Wesson Schofield 45's and none of them voiced their concern of Jeb's rudeness. Waiting until Jeb was satisfied he had marked everything he would mark, I asked my Australian friend, "Want some grub?"

Jeb wagging his tail ran up the 4 wooden steps then planted his end gate on the boardwalk. Then he tilted his head giving me his "whatcha waiting for look." Shaking my head like I seemed to do a lot when responding to Jeb's antics, I dismounted and tied off Cinders to the one and only hitching post in Cimarron. Palming my Schofield's one at a time, I checked my loads. I was not hunting trouble, but somehow trouble more likely than not - found me. Satisfied I was ready for anything that could be thrown my way, I climbed the stairs. Once on the boardwalk in front of the Elk Saloon I bent down and looked Jeb in the eye before speaking, "I know you are hungrier that a woodpecker with a headache, but try not to make a mess of things in here."

Jeb gives me that quizzical look that only Jeb could give before we pushed through the Batwing doors of the Elk Saloon. The saloon was busy with the usual folks that made or were trying to make their living and fortunes here along the Rocky Mountain frontier. There were miners, cowboys, gamblers, railroad workers, Orientals, and the painted ladies. Luckily there was an empty table with 3 chairs—so we took it and planted our butts down.

Jeb took the chair directly in front of me and his eyes darted here and there through-out the room as he took a gander at all the gents and ladies inside the saloon. A bald-headed man with a sizable unkempt mustache told us what was on the spit out back and on the menu. It would seem that turkey, taters, and a slice of sorghum cake was only items on the bill of fare. After ordering our meal and a shot of whiskey for me, a bowl of water for Jeb, and since I was almost civilized, a glass of water for me. The bald-headed bar keep returned quickly with our drinks and the meal. I gave up trying to slow Jeb down as he wolfed down the turkey, tater, and cake. As usual, trying to get him not to make a mess of things - had failed. Looking about at the other patrons of this establishment, it would seem Jeb's table manners were on par with the rest of the clientele of the Elk Saloon.

After finishing up my fare, I tapped my belly and there was a loud "thunk" showing there was no more room. Jeb just like always when full of grub curled up in his chair and promptly fell asleep. Catching the bald-headed barkeep's eye, I showed I wanted another shot of whisky. Facing the batwing doors and the front of the saloon, I saw a white-bearded mountain of a man walk through them like he owned the place. His sheer size alone caught everyone's attention as they all turned to look at the mountain man legend himself - RJ Schwartz.

I had known RJ since I was 10-years-old; he was kin by marriage. His wife was a Ute Indian woman who was a cousin of my mother Walk With Ghost. My mother was a princess of the Grand River Utes in Kawuneeche Valley in the Middle Park region of Colorado up north of here. RJ had to be in his upper 60s. The mountain man was sizable at 6'4" and weighing in at 260 pounds. RJ's wife and son died of the fever when I was 14. Only days after their death he left the village and made his way into the mountains out of grief for all he had lost. Over the years I had heard tales of his exploits along the timberline and just like my step-father Matt Lee known as Ghost, RJ became a legend. I had not seen him in 15 years - until now.

The only empty seat in the Elk Saloon was at our table and RJ saw it and headed towards it. Once he was 20 feet away, he looked at me and he stopped dead in his tracks as he was running my face through his thinker. Several seconds later, a gigantic smile crossed his face that matched mine. In a half chuckle RJ said, "By the Lord Almighty, if it ain't the little pissant Dale Lee Patton! No longer a child, but a man, and if the stories are true, a man to be reckoned with. "

RJ sized me up for a few seconds looking at me—not as the boy he knew, but as the man I had become. His eyes showed he liked what he saw before he spoke again, "You have the look of your mother, and the tall and stout frame of your father, Guy Patton. But, what I sense most about you Dale is the confidence, and strength of your step daddy Matt Lee. Seeing you now and knowing you step-dad Ghost, I never doubted the stories I have heard about you being hell on wheels with those Smith & Wesson's you carry so proudly. I see in your eyes, son, that if anyone was fool enough to brace you, they would find that they had a catamount by the tail."

Pointing at Jeb, and then reaching and giving Jeb a hardy tussle of his ears, he added, "And this feller here must be that ugly mutt that runs with you."

Jeb although he had just been insulted rolled into RJ's good-sized hand for more loving. Jeb had already had become fast friends with the enormous mountain man. Pointing at the extra chair, I said, "Take a seat RJ. You have no idea how good it is to see you. With you standing here, a flash of memories just sputtered through my mind of all the things you and Ghost taught me when I was a pup."

Although I was not sure they had built the chair for the man of RJ's heft, it seemed to be under no strain after RJ quickly settle in. Still smiling RJ took some more time looking me up and down before he spoke, "Still hard to believe that the young Dale Lee Patton, the legendary Patton the bounty hunter is now sitting here before me. Like I said, I never doubted the rumors and now I know them to be true that you have grown horns and is tough as a whetstone. Some say the Schofield's you carry are like lightning in your hands, much like Ghost, Lucas Eldridge, and Chance Bondurant. I also heard a tale you had lost your wife and because of that you have become the most feared bounty hunter along the timberline. If you are a bounty hunter, you must be here for the Grizz!"

Waving the barkeep over, I told him, "I am sure my friend here is hungrier than a bitch wolf with fallen arches. Set him up with the same fixings that my Australian friend and I just had and also a round of whiskey—except for the dog—he has had his limit."

The bald-headed barkeep smiled and said, "Right away, sir." As he hustled off, I leaned my elbows onto the table and replied to RJ in a serious tone, "I lost my wife, and as you know I probably will never recover from that. Sold my ranch over near Gunnison, and I bounty hunt for a living now. Jeb and I wandered into Cimarron looking for a sheriff's office to thumb through some wanted posters. At the moment we are unemployed. I know nothing about the - Grizz. Is that a man or a critter?"

CHAPTER 2

RJ leaned back in his chair and when he spoke he matched my serious tone, "Some around here say he is neither man nor beast. That this grizzly bear is the devil reincarnated. The local Mexicans around started calling the creature Diablo - devil - in Spanish, and the name has taken hold. Others believe that Diablo is not the devil, but is an evil spirit that roams the Black Canyon in the form of a one-eyed grizzly bear that comes out of the night and preys on the helpless. The Ute Indians have always had their superstitions and thought there was an evil presence within the Black Canyon and that it is has now taken the body of this grizzly bear to wreck devastation on all that wander the canyon. I have my own thoughts on the beast, but what is important to know is that there is a $5000 bounty on Diablo."

The bald-headed barkeep returned with RJ's supper and our drinks just as RJ finished telling me about Diablo. As RJ wolfed his supper down, he seemed to have the same table manners of Jeb. Looking at Jeb's reaction to RJ; I could not determine if the dingo was pleased to have met someone that matched his etiquette skills or they disgusted him. Watching Jeb watch RJ was about as entertaining as it gets.

Rolling around what RJ had said about the grizzly bear in my thinker waiting for RJ to finish his meal, I had several thoughts. A $5000 bounty was unheard of, and I could not even imagine someone backs that much cash or gold for a grizzly bear. If that sum of money was true. How come so much? And if it was true; there had to be more than a few men hunting this bear for the bounty. More people on the hunt meant more people in the woods. It would be a race to find and kill the bear. I didn't cotton to the idea of being in a race for a bounty. To be rushed in the bounty hunting business could cause you to make mistakes; mistakes that get you killed.

RJ finished up his turkey and taters and leaned back with a smile and satisfied look on his face. In the 15 years since I had seen RJ he had aged, his eyes had lost a little of life's spark, but his smile was the same. RJ's gray hair was long and past his shoulders, his shaggy gray whiskers hung down to the center of his chest. He was dressed in a fringed buckskin pants and shirt. If I didn't know better, I would say they were the same buckskins I last saw him in 15 years ago. Looking at my friend from long ago—wanting more answers on the bounty for Diablo. I asked, "A $5000 bounty is a fortune. Why so much? Who is backing that impressive sum for the bounty?"

RJ stroked his beard when he spoke, "The Denver and Rio Grande railroad put up $2500. And Captain W. M. Cline matched the amount with his own $2500. The railroad has lost 12 of their workers over the last 4 months to the one-eyed Diablo during the construction of their railroad through the Black Canyon. The workers are now too afraid to enter the canyon to maintain the tracks, so Denver and Rio Grande is hoping this bounty will rid themselves of the grizzly that has cost them so much in manpower and money. Captain W. M. Cline owns the largest cattle ranch in the area. The Cline ranch is located just outside of Cimarron, at the confluence of Cimarron Creek and the Little Cimarron River. The Captain has lost cattle and recently his eldest son to the demon bear. His son tracked Diablo into the canyon a month ago, the horse he was riding returned to the ranch 3 days later minus the son. It is feared he met the same fate as the unfortunate railroad workers. This grizzly is huge, those that have seen him say he weighs about 900 pounds and standing on his hind feet he is 9 feet tall. With Diablo missing his right eye, he is loaded to the muzzle with rage."

Sitting back into my chair, I pondered on what RJ had just said. It would appear that the bounty of $5000 was legit, with backing from 2 different sources that would seem to have plenty of money. If the grizzly bear had in fact killed at least 13 men in 4 months, Diablo was doing it for the sake of killing and not necessarily for food. If Diablo had only one eye, he had probably lost the other eye because of some run in with a man. Bears like most critters shy away from encounters with men unless they are cornered, starving, or killing for revenge the only way a grizzly can. Grizzly bears were smart and it would seem this one was roaming the canyon and killing for the sheer pleasure of killing men. My gut instinct was telling me that this bear, this canyon, was something maybe Jeb and I should avoid.

The Black Canyon was named so, because of the way it was formed. A lot of the canyon only saw sunlight for about a half hour each day. My ancestors the Ute Indians had known the canyon to exist for a long time before the first Europeans saw it. They referred to the river that cut the canyon now known as the Gunnison River as "much rocks, big water," and are known, even to this day, to avoid the canyon out of superstition; that evil spirits roamed within the canyon walls. I had traveled the length of the Black Canyon years ago, and I felt what my ancestors felt. Maybe it was only stories that were told to children to scare them, maybe not. For whatever reason, I never wanted to go back—it just seemed like bad luck to me. A man killing bear within the walls of that canyon seemed like bad destiny and fate to me.

RJ was still giving my dingo some loving by scratching him behind the ears when I leaned onto the table and said, "A $5000 bounty will put a lot of men in the woods; all rushing to take the head of Diablo before anyone else can. Too many men, too many guns, all going after the same prize will get some of them killed. Last time Jeb and I hunted a critter for bounty, a killer wolf, it about put us both under. I think Jeb and I will pass on this one and stick to hunting men."

By the look on the aging mountain man's face, you would have thought I had just stabbed him in the heart. RJ quit petting Jeb and showed his disappointment in how he slouched his shoulders. Maybe he thought I was a coward. The hunting of Diablo just didn't feel right. RJ Schwartz, a man I respected and loved, leaned forward and in a voice just above a whisper said, "Dale, I need you to partner up with me on this. We will split the bounty; half for you and half for me. Between the 2 of us I believe we would have a better chance of bagging this monster than any of those other yahoo's that will go for the grizzly. As a favor to an old friend, I need you to do this with me."

I was confused by what RJ had just said. RJ Schwartz, the legendary mountain man, never needed or wanted help from any man or woman—ever. Just as that thought bounced around in my thinker, RJ continued, "Dale, I sit here before you a shell of what I once was. If my reckoning is correct, I am 64 years-old. I can't hear, can't see, can't smell, can't sleep through the night without pissing twice, and can't fight like I used too. And sure as hell can't please a woman anymore. I have nothing, except my horse, rifle, pistol, and the clothes on my back. I own a small cabin near Lake City, Colorado, but have no money to live on. Diablo will be my last glorious adventure in life that will give me the money to lie low until the good Lord calls me home. I know my weaknesses now and I can't take Diablo on my own. Seeing you here today unexpectedly was heaven sent. I know that now. I need this ugly mutt of yours, I need you Dale."

Looking at this man I knew so well. He was in a roundabout way related to me, he and Matt Lee had taught me the ways of the mountains. He helped teach me the love of nature and how to be one with it. There was no denying I loved this man as if he was my father. If RJ Schwartz thought he needed my help; I could not refuse him. My gut instinct was saying—no. Doing what was right by this man was telling me - yes. Slowly nodding my head "yes" I spoke in a simple voice, "Okay RJ, you got Jeb and I as partners. We will hunt down Diablo together."

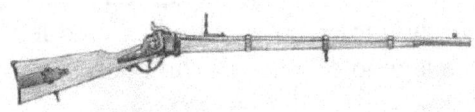

CHAPTER 3

The following morning and still feeling a tad bit uneasy about the prospect of hunting Diablo in the Black Canyon, Jeb and I met RJ at a merchandise tent on the major road of Cimarron. RJ carried a 50 caliber Hawking rifle for large game such as moose, buffalo, or a bear. I had no such weapon and RJ knew a fellow selling a 50-90 Sharps rifle. The 50-90 Sharps cartridge is a black powder round introduced in 1877 by the Sharps Rifle Manufacturing Company.

The 50-90 Sharps rifle with a 30 inch barrel was a new weapon, but had already reached legendary status because of a man named Billy Dixon. Dixon is a scout and buffalo hunter active in the Texas Panhandle. Just 4 months ago during the Second Battle of Adobe Walls. The outpost of 28 men and women was attacked by a band of more than a 1000 Indians. The stand-off continued into a third day, when a group of Indians were noticed about a mile east of Adobe Walls. The story goes that Dixon took aim with his 50-90 Sharps buffalo rifle. He knocked an Indian off his horse, killing him. Unnerved, the Indians then withdrew and left the settlement alone. Or so the legend of Billy Dixon goes.

The Sharps was expensive and cost $50 gold and my spare pistol - a fairly new single action Colt 45. But, if Diablo was as dangerous as his reputation, I needed to be properly armed for him. Since the Sharps was a long range weapon, I hoped that we would take him from a distance. I didn't cotton to the idea of being up close with a 900 pound man-killing grizzly bear. I had to pitch in another $2 for another rifle scabbard to house the new Sharps.

After outfitting myself with the long range bear rifle, we moved on down the road a piece until we came to another merchandise tent selling supplies. After splitting the cost for enough venison jerky, hardtack, fat-backed bacon, salt pork, salt, flour, beans, hominy, sugar, and canned apples for at least 10 days in the field. Once RJ and I thought we were outfitted properly for a grizzly hunt, we readied our horses.

Cinders my blood bay mare was easy enough, I just had to add the extra scabbard for the Sharps rifle. RJ had 2 horses, both were paints. Tala his riding horse was a big mare standing nearly 19 hands, more black than white. A stout horse for carrying a sizeable man, which RJ was. Nina was his pack horse and smaller than Tala at 17 hands and was more white than brown. Both horses were well muscled and well taken care of. After loading all the supplies, gear, and weapons, we started out for the mouth of the Black Canyon.

We moved towards the Black Canyon through a smaller unnamed canyon heading northwest, staying in the shadow of Sheep Knob Mountain lurking in the west. The day as it progressed cooled considerably as the summer sun disappeared behind dark clouds that seemed bloated with rain.

We stopped once and let the horses and Jeb get their fill of spring water that was oozing from the side of the hill. As we surveyed the storm clouds filled with rain overhead and the encroaching darkness of the night, RJ and I each ate about a ½ of a pound of venison jerky and some hardtack. After the horses had finished their drink RJ said, "The Gunnison River is about another hour, we will hear it long before we see it."

We moved cautiously towards the Black Canyon. You could feel the tension of Jeb, Cinders, Tala, Nina, RJ and myself. It was as if we all knew we had entered hostile territory. My Ute Indian heritage and my gut instinct was giving me all the warnings signs.

Just like when I was in the canyon once before, I could feel an unsettled presence among the rocks and the trees. My ancestors felt it and so did I. I knew - spirits lived here, but not the friendly spirits.

RJ had been right - we heard the Gunnison River long before we saw it. We entered a gorge, remote from the sun, where the walls and the rocks were two thousand feet sheer, and where a rock-splintered river roared and howled ten feet below a track which seemed to have been built on the simple principle of dropping wagon after wagon of dirt into the river and pinning a few rails a-top. There was a glory, wonder, and a mystery about the canyon and this river. We finally crossed the narrow-gauge railroad track that snaked along the west side of the river. Stepping over the tracks, we rode up to the sheer drop off bank of the mighty Gunnison River. I had forgotten the sound of this river. The Ute's called it "much rocks, big water" and there was no better fitting description that I could come up with. The fast rushing water was so deafening it almost sounded like a freight train. Flowing east to west through the almost 50 miles of the Black Canyon the river dropped 34 feet per mile which created a river flowing so fast and dangerous that there was no way in hell we could ever cross it to the other side.

RJ pointed to the sky, and he shouted, but I could barely hear him above the ear shattering wailing flow of the river when he said, "We need to find shelter before the sky opens up on us."

Just before sundown we were lucky enough to find a shallow cave that was 10 to 12 feet deep and big enough with enough headroom for our horses. RJ gathered what we needed for a fire while I took care of the horses. Jeb seemed a tad confused and nervous as he stood guard over all of us. The roar of the Gunnison River had to be harsh for his dingo keen sense of hearing.

Cinders, Tala, and Nina all got the same grooming with a good brush down with my wooden curry comb after I had unsaddled them. Showing the horses the love they deserved, I gave each of them a pinch of sugar as a treat. Not feeling the need to hobble them since the brewing storm overhead would keep them close to the fire tonight.

After RJ had gotten the cook fire going - he had the fixings of fat-backed bacon and beans all ready for Jeb and I once the horses were taken care of.

Once we started to eat the sky opened up with a hellish storm. Our shallow cave gave us ample protection from the wind and the pounding rain. The temperature had dropped and the now night air had a chill to it. Once the rain started, so did the lightning and thunder. A thundering explosion immediately followed each lightning bolt telling us we were at the center of the storm. With each crash of thunder and combined with the roar of the river, it was deafening. RJ and I didn't speak, for it would have been useless.

Jeb had moved close enough to me that his back was touching my leg as he starred northward into the wall of water as the storm raged. With the enclosed feeling of the canyon walls topped off with the howl of the storm and river, the dingo must have needed the comfort of being close to me. I know I needed the comfort from him.

Another thought crossed my mind, and I caught RJ's attention by waving my hand. Once he was looking at me I pointed in the river's direction and then flattened out my palm of my hand and raised it slowly in front of me. My intent was to show that with all the rain the river would raise and there would be a possibility of flooding. My thought was maybe our shelter out of the storm had not been as well thought out as it should have been. RJ smiled in the way I used to remember him doing so. He shrugged his shoulders as if to say "it is too late now" and he went back to cleaning his pistols and his Hawkins rifle. Seeing RJ's wisdom of the moment - I cleaned my own Smith & Wesson Schofield 45's, and my new Sharp's rifle.

Every few minutes I would follow Jeb's line of sight as he gazed into the darkness and rain. Not sure what was on the Australian dingo's mind, but I could not help but wonder if Diablo the 900 pound man-killing grizzly was hunkered down out of the rain or if he had forsaken the storm and was hunting his next victim.

I could not shake the feeling of foreboding that had ridden with me since we started on this trail. Trying to push any uneasiness to the back of my thinker was not working—bad thoughts, evil spirits kept racing through my mind. If it had not been for RJ; at first light I would pack up everything and take Jeb and head out of this ominous place of swirling dire omens. A $5000 dollar bounty was a heap load of money. Money or not, if it had not been for the plea of my dear friend RJ - I would just ride away. RJ Schwartz the legendary mountain man's words kept buzzing through my mind, "Diablo will be my last glorious adventure in life that will give me the money to lie low until the good Lord calls me home."

Looking pass the campfire into the darkness and the rain—I felt whatever awaited us out there was death, decay, and malevolent.

-

CHAPTER 4

The night passed slowly as the rain and thunder continued. I woke up twice and looked to Jeb as he laid next to me for any sign of danger. Every time I woke Jeb was looking out pass the campfire into the unknown. The horses had stayed close to the fire and out of the rain, as I knew they would.

When I woke the 3rd time the rain and thunder had stopped, but the river raged on. What little I could see of the night sky up through the narrow walls of the canyon was clear. The fire had long died out and the only light was that given off by the few stars twinkling above. Jeb had finally fallen into a deep sleep. RJ was fast asleep. With Jeb out cold, and the horses seemed content, I fell back into a peaceful sleep.

Waking up an hour before sunup and the misty air was fresh and cool. The morning after a night of rain there was always dew left on the evergreen and aspen leaves. The mountain grass was also heavy with morning dew and the horses were already moving about and grazing. RJ had woken up before me and had already stirred what remained of the fire from last night, bringing the still hot embers to the surface to feed on the kindling he placed on top.

As Jeb and I stood and stretched the kinks out of our backs I asked the aging mountain man, "What's the plan old man?"

RJ smiled as he built the fire into a cooking one, "After some grub will head westward toward Montrose following the river until we run across any sign of Diablo. Once we got scent, then we set your hound loose and track and kill the bastard!"

Following the river would be easy enough since the canyon was so narrow that was all you could do. Shaking my head—yes—I said in a chuckle, "Sounds simple enough even a Patton could remember and follow that plan."

The dawn of a fresh day had lighten the canyon some, but the sheer 2000 foot rocky walls would prevent sunlight from reaching us most of the day. After a filling breakfast and getting the horses ready we started out moving westward through the blacken canyon as we began our hunt for Diablo. Since this hunt was RJ's soiree, he was first on the trail riding Tala, with Nina the packhorse reins tied to his saddle. I brought up the rear, riding my mare Cinders. Jeb alternated in between being by my side if the width of the trail allowed it or in front if it did not.

Because of the low light, the shadows played tricks on my mind. It was as if there were apparitions behind every tree. It made me realize even more why my ancestors thought the Black Canyon was a home of evil spirits. I tried to push the stories of my youth to the back of my mind, telling myself they were just stories to scare youngsters. Every time I would shake the eerie feeling of the canyon, another abnormal shadow would appear behind a rock or tree.

The level of sound in the canyon had diminished since the thunder and lightning had moved out last night. But the rumble of the Gunnison River was constant as we trailed along the river and the narrow-gauge railroad tracks.

The canyon seemed to act like a natural sluice regarding the mountain wind. Just like the one and only time I had ever been in the Black Canyon, the wind was steady from east to west as we traveled westward. Which was only an issue if danger or any scent that it may have was in front of us, then Jeb and the horses could not detect it. If the scent of a threat was behind us, we would get plenty of warning.

It was midmorning when we found the trail of the beast we hunted in the form of Tony DeLorger. DeLorger was a bounty hunter much like myself and it would seem he had been hunting Diablo just like we were for the hefty bounty. DeLorger and his horse lives had ended here in the Black Canyon. And by the looks of the kill site, it was the work of the beast we were hunting.

Grizzly bears are opportunistic hunters and feeders. They will take advantage of any food source when they have the opportunity to do so. In most attacks, grizzlies will not usually pursue their prey over long distances, but preferred to attack from ambush. Grizzlies, because of their size, normally attack their prey from the top of the animal. This had all proven true with what were the remains of DeLorger and his horse.

I never liked DeLorger. He was a braggart and thought he was smarter than everyone else. He was a despicable man when it came to women. Tony thought everyone else was beneath him. Even though I did not care for the man I would never wish the death that he experienced on anyone. Just before sundown and the rain last night Diablo had surprised the bounty hunter before he could fire any of his pistols or rifles. Studying the tracks, it would seem the killer grizzly had been upwind and ambushed the bounty hunter. Although Diablo weighed in about 900 pounds, he could outrun any man in a 20 yard race. DeLorger had tried to fend off the savage attack using only his bowie knife and had lost not only his life, but his right arm that still held the bowie knife. His head and upper body and been so savaged by Diablo the only way I could recognize the man I had known was by the distinctive fringed buckskins he wore. His horse had been feasted on as the mares' withers tissue was gone. The withers of any animal seemed to be chosen meat for grizzlies.

RJ and I carefully studied the kill site, trying to get a feel for our adversary. Every few minutes we would look at each other and sort of shake our heads. Diablo was not an ordinary grizzly. Diablo was cunning and smarter than any other bear I had ever encountered before. If RJ and I had any brains we just hightail it out of the canyon and leave this grizzly bear be. Problem was, there was no backup in either of us. That probably was not the best thing.

Jeb scurried here and there over the kill site as he was getting the scent he needed to trail the demon bear. The rain last night had washed away any tracks, but had not washed away all the scent. I knew that the dingo could track the grizzly.

Jeb was almost prancing as he was more than ready to begin the hunt. The coppery smell of blood and the scent of the grizzly had set him on edge. I lowered myself to Jeb's height, and I reached out and grabbed his head gently and brought him closer to me and whispered to him, "Listen my Australian friend, this grizzly is nothing to fool around with. He will be quicker than you can imagine and one swipe from his paws and you will be done for. This I cannot abide. I would hate to lose my best friend on this bounty so promise me Jeb you will do nothing foolish when it comes to Diablo!"

My dingo and partner calmed down and finally planted his butt to listen as I tried to reason with him. I could see in his eyes he knew this talk was important, he might not understand everything I said, but he got the drift of what I was trying to convey. When I quit talking, we looked into each other's eyes for a spell and Jeb finally lowered his ears and leaned forward and licked my face. I pulled him in tighter and held him for a minute showing my love for him then I let him go and said, "Now that you got your mind focused on the job ahead, let's begin the hunt."

CHAPTER 5

Not knowing if DeLorger was a Christian or not we still gave him a Christian burial. RJ even sang the song Amazing Grace. It was the best we could do for someone we hardly knew. If DeLorger had a problem with that, he could take it up with us in the hereafter.

After checking our weapons I let Jeb do his job and released telling him, "Go find us a grizzly my friend."

Dingo's much like the timber wolf has the ability to tell the difference between mankind or animal scent, and that sets them apart in our natural world as superb hunters.

I had learned to rely on the dingo, and we built our relationship on trust. Jeb knew he could not start trailing the scent in any manner he saw fit. We had learned to work together with a mutual understanding of each of our limitations.

The amount of odor left by Diablo depended on several factors, such as fear or anger; exertion; and or if he was healthy or not. My job was to keep Jeb on Diablos scent and not let him wander off in search of any badger, elk, rabbit, or any other critter that crossed scents with the grizzly.

It was my belief that scent was hard to trail in areas that have little to no vegetation, however, scent will still collect in areas that might keep it from moving or being destroyed. Cool, shady areas — such as beneath large stands of evergreens and aspen trees — hold scent far better than flat, open tracks of hard surfaces subject to the blistering summer sun.

Jeb when trailing a scent usually kept his head closer to the ground with his ears straight back, if the scent became weaker he would lift his head higher and his ears would almost stand straight up. If the dingo moved with impatience in and out of the scent trail, I knew he had crossed several scents other than just the one we were hunting. Jeb used his natural ability to hunt with his nose.

I hunted with my eyes. Grizzly bears especially one the size of Diablo's tracks were similar to a man with 5 toes, but much larger. The major difference between a black bear track's and a grizzly track is that grizzlies have long claws extending up to 4 inches, where the black bear's claws were much shorter. A better indicator is that black bears have slightly separated toes, while grizzlies' toes are usually joined together.

There were tree markings along the scent trail showing that Diablo had marked his territory. Bears mark their territory by biting or scraping trees. Some bears will mark the same trees repeatedly. Some trees may be scratched by numerous bears, or repeatedly by the same bear, over the years. Some bear marks can permanently scar tree bark.

From time to time during the hunt we ran across grizzly bear scat. Bear scat we located was in piles. Each time we located fresh scat, Jeb would spend a full minute getting a fresh scent.

Jeb and I worked together as a team and RJ sort of held back now that we had working scent trail following Jeb and I letting us do our job. RJ as we moved steadily on the trail of Diablo rode with his Hawkins bear rifle cross ways across his saddle.

We moved through the evergreen and aspen tree line that ran across the bottom of the sheer cliffs of the canyon and never over 50 yards from the narrow-gauge railroad tracks and 60 yards from the Gunnison River. The constant reverberation of the river left RJ and myself no choice, but not to talk to one another. Any words spoken were drowned out by the roar of the river. It also made it difficult for me to command Jeb and keep him focused on the task of just tracking Diablo. Luckily Jeb would stop once in a while and look back at me so I could give him hand signals. Obviously without being able to speak to Jeb made our undertaking just that much harder.

Midafternoon the Black Canyon was still dark and dreary. Not from cloud cover, but from the sun's inability to reach the bottom of the canyon due to the lofty height of the crumbling rock walls. The shadows continued to play tricks on my mind. There was no rhyme or reason on the lengths to the shadows. Some shadows were longer than others, some leaned left and others leaned right, all the shadows seemed catawampus to what nature intended. Nothing felt as it should be and passaging time here seemed to be at a standstill. My feelings of foreboding had been increasing as we moved further into the canyon as we hunted the grizzly known as Diablo.

Pulling back on Cinders reins, I brought her to a halt. Jeb had stopped and lifted his head as if he was no longer trailing Diablos scent, but trying to catch a whiff in the canyon air. Looking back at RJ, he sort of just shrugged his shoulders as we both waited on Jeb to continue tracking.

Jeb lowered his head and then would raise it almost immediately as he started to move in an ever-widening circle. It would seem the dingo had lost the scent of the grizzly. Dismounting Cinders, I searched the ever present shadows for anything out of kilter. Which did me no good in this godforsaken canyon since everything was out of kilter. With both eyes searching the trees and shadows, I dragged my Sharps from the scabbard. RJ had already dismounted and held his Hawkins bear rifle in his hands and he searched the back trail.

RJ and I both could not talk because of the continuing thunder of water rushing over enormous boulders of the Gunnison River just to the north of us. Something was amiss for sure and I was still a tad baffled by this new circumstance. My gut instinct was doing double time and making my heart race.

As Jeb tried in vain to catch the scent of Diablo, he was having no luck as his circle of confusion continued. Keeping the shadows of the nearby trees in observation, I meandered inside of Jeb's ever-widening circle and tried to see if there was any sign of the grizzly we had been following. There was nothing. It was as if the

Diablo had just disappeared. My mind told me there was no way in hell a 900 pound grizzly could just disappear without a trace, but that is what seems to have happened.

Something didn't feel right, there was something different from before. This damn canyon and its tricks on my thinker had my mind buzzing, looking for a sign, looking for clues. Then it hit me like a shovel to the head. Looking westward, then skyward, then eastward—it was the wind. The wind had changed—it was no longer blowing east to west. The canyon wind had reversed and now was blowing west to east. Why there was no more scent in front of us is because the demon bear was no longer in front of us—he was now behind us using the wind to hide his scent. Diablo as cunning as he was had used the mountain wind to his advantage. We were no longer the hunters; we had now become the hunted.

I needed to warn RJ that Diablo was now behind us and to be on the look-out, but the rumbling of the Gunnison River was so loud, he would never hear me. I waved my right arm trying to get his attention and finally RJ looked over his shoulder at me and smiled that famous RJ smile. Looking past RJ, I saw one of the tree shadows move forward in the dim light of the canyon. The shadow moved quickly and took the form of a grizzly bear. A grizzly bear attacking his prey. Diablo was close, too close to RJ. Raising my Sharps, I aimed it above RJ's right shoulder as Diablo moved in for the kill. RJ's smiled vanished as he saw me raising the Sharps and then he realized what was happening, he spun around trying to bring his Hawkins rifle to his shoulder. I fired first.

It was Diablo, for his right eye was missing. My slug took Diablo in the upper left shoulder as he raised up to his full height just before his massive right paw clawed into RJ's upper body. RJ's right trigger finger twitched and the Hawkins rifle fired - into the dirt just to the side of the grizzly.

The half-blinded Diablo was wounded and enraged as he continued his savage attack on my lifelong friend. RJ during the initial attack had quickly dropped the now useless Hawkins and still had the wherewithal and pulled his 12" Bowie. With 2 vicious thrusts, he stabbed Diablo just below his left shoulder. All 12" of the blade drove deep into the flesh of the grizzly, but just like me shooting him - the knife plunges only seem to piss off Diablo even more. The coppery smell of blood quickly filled the air, so much in fact I could taste it.

As I shucked my now empty Sharps to the side I fast-palmed both of my Schofield 45's as Jeb rushed the bear in a vain attempt to save RJ. Diablo acted as if Jeb was not even there and continued mauling RJ. At first I was afraid to fire in case I hit RJ as the infuriated bear had RJ's neck in his powerful jaws and was swinging his body back and forth as if he was intent on tearing the mountain man in two.

Realizing at this point accidentally shooting RJ was not even a concern anymore. This mauling by Diablo - RJ my friend would not survive. Firing 3 times with my right pistol hitting the grizzly twice in the head just below his blinded right eye. The third shot missed. The 2nd slug struck home got Diablo's attention, and he stopped thrashing my friend's body back and forth. With RJ still clenched within his jaws, the half-blind grizzly looked at me as Jeb ran back and forth barking at the 900 pound bear. At this point Diablo had been stabbed twice, and had been shot 3 times, once with a 50 caliber Sharps. Jeb was of no concern to him, but the bear looked at me. The intelligence I saw in his left eye was astounding to me. Not wanting the grizzly to catch a second wind before he died and rush me and give me the same fate as RJ - I raised my right-hand pistol and took aim. Firing once, I shot the devil grizzly in his left eye.

After the 45 slug penetrated Diablo's left eye, it exploded into his brain. The now fully blinded bear dropped RJ's body and stood shakily to his full height. Which scared the crap out of me. I emptied the last 2 shells of my right-handed Schofield into the center chest area of the demon bear, hoping to hit his heart—if he had a heart.

Diablo sat down on his butt—hard. His massive arms and paws collapsed as he started the last stage of dying before my eyes. His colossal head slumped to his chest, and I saw him take his last breath as he fell to his right onto his side. There had been no last sigh or roar from the gigantic bear—if there had been—it would not have been heard. Any last sound from the killer bear would have been drowned out from the constant thunder from the fast flowing Gunnison River just 30 yards away.

With a heavy heart, I sat down next to the body of RJ. The darkness of the canyon was overpowering as the shadows shifted once again in ways that nature never intended. The sound of rushing and crashing water over the boulders in the Gunnison River left me voiceless. Reaching out, I touched what remained of my friend and was overcome with grief. For those that think men of the mountains never cry, never saw one all alone in the dark holding on to the body of one they loved. The tears flowed, and they flowed.

Jeb, stunned with emotion with the death of our friend, curled up into my lap as we mourned the death of RJ Schwartz, the legendary mountain man.

PATTON BOUNTY HUNTER 5th Adventure

CHAPTER 1

Jeb, the cinnamon-colored short-haired Australian born dingo, took point as we headed into the mining camp of Maysville, Colorado. It always excited Jeb when we would reach a town or mining camp along the Rocky Mountain frontier. If I had not known better, I would say Jeb was born a town dog instead of being born in the Outback of Australia. He liked to strut his fancy up and down the main street of any town. Which I would not have minded one bit, except he likes to mark the town as if he owned it by peeing on every hitching post, tree, buckboard, stairs, and boardwalk. If any horse or man was standing still - they got peed on as well. More than a few horses or townsfolk tried to kick Jeb once they got marked, but the dingo was too fast for them and dodge every ill-timed kick. Jeb would pee then scurry on down the road with that dingo grin of his. When folks would give me the ole' stink eye when Jeb fouled their pant legs or boots I would just shrug my shoulders like I didn't know whose damn dog he was. Folks knew better but after glimpsing my 2 Smith & Wesson Schofield 45's that were belted on my waist they quickly decided a little yellow-colored dingo water was not that bad.

This was my 2nd trip to Maysville in the last week. Just 6 days ago I was here picking up a $400 wanted poster on a man named Rick Mitchell. Today's excursion into town was to claim that bounty. Mitchell was riding sideways across his horse, which was tied off to my saddle on Cinders, my blood bay three-year-old mare. Mitchell had been wanted on the western slope of the Rocky Mountains for various offences. The worse one being he killed 2 men right here in Maysville in the Mountain Man Saloon with a 12 inch Bowie knife over an altercation playing 5-card stud. Rick Mitchell was a man to be reckoned with when it came to knife fighting. Not the brightest individual when I caught up with him and he brought his 12 inch Bowie knife to a gunfight.

Maysville was the conglomeration of two small camps located right next to each other. One named Crazy Camp and the other Maysville. When they merged, the town took on the name of Maysville. Maysville sat at the Eastern Junction of Monarch Pass. Just like most mining camps on the western slope of the Rockies it was a boomtown with dance halls, large supply stores, 2 hotels, and a half dozen saloons, and one sheriff office with a good size jailhouse. My intended destination was the sheriff's office to drop off the body of the now deceased Rick Mitchell and put in a claim for the $400 bounty.

After tying Cinders off to the hitching post in front of the law-dogs office, Jeb went straight through the open front door to say howdy to Richard Paulson, Maysville sheriff. Booming laughter erupted from inside as sheriff Paulson stated in his booming voice, "Well hell, if it isn't my favorite Rocky Mountain critter—Jeb the bounty hunter!"

Stepping through the door, my eyes quickly adjusted to the dim light inside the small and cramp room. Jeb was sitting on Sheriff's Paulson lap with the older white-haired law officer was grinning from ear to ear petting the dingo. Paulson laughed again and stated in his not so quiet voice, "Well Jeb my good friend, it seems you brought your sidekick whatshisname."

Chuckling as I sat down in the only other chair in the room I said, "That damn dingo has more friends than I do."

Paulson still amused replied, "Of course he does Dale, he is smarter and way more handsome than you are."

Paulson with one last tussle of Jeb's right ear he sat Jeb back on to the floor and looked at me and said in a more serious tone, "As glad as I am to see you both Dale, I take it that this is not a social call."

Standing up, I said, "I got Rick Mitchell outside. He did not come peacefully."

After the undertaker had relieved me of the body of Rick Mitchell I filled out the proper paperwork to put in a claim on the $400. Having done that sheriff Paulson and I smoked a couple of hand-rolled cigars as Jeb slept in the chair next to the sheriff. Enjoying the smoke and the peace and quiet, Paulson's eyes lit up, and he said, "I damn near forgot. There is someone in town looking to talk to you. And believe me, Patton, you are not going to want to pass on talking to them."

Flicking my ash on to the floor I let what the sheriff had said roll around in my thinker for a minute before curiosity had got the best of me, "First off Richard, how would anyone know I would be in Maysville? Do you know what they want to talk to me about or why would I not want to pass on talking to them?"

Paulson face split with a smile when he heard my questions, and in his deep baritone voice replied, "How they knew you be here— is because I told them you would be back within a week or two claiming the bounty on Mitchell. They did not divulge why they wanted to talk to you, but were adamant that it was you they wanted to speak with. The reason my good friend you don't want to pass talking to them is because 'one of them' is a woman no less and a stunner to look at. A very capable and beautiful blue-eyed blonde."

Now I was in a total bewilderment. Why would a beautiful woman want with me? And why would she be willing to stick around town for several weeks to get the opportunity to speak with me? In the business of being a bounty hunter—it did not warm my heart any when I hear someone has been waiting around to see you. That could only be bad news. A wife or a lover of someone I had possibly killed or collected a bounty on? Something else that the sheriff had said struck me as a little off kilter is that he used the word—capable. Flicking another set of ashes on to the floor, I asked, "What do you mean when you say she is capable?"

Sheriff Paulson was still grinning when he answered, "Stunning she is, but she is no princess. No fancy dresses or jewelry, she wears button down Levi's, dusty boots, and a cattleman creased Stetson. She rides her horse like the wind, and she wears a strapped down holster that houses a Colt army revolver. I feel she knows how to use it. All in all - with all that rolled into one woman, I call that capable."

I did not like it one bit. Sounded like some sort of set-up to me - maybe an ambush. If it is an ambush of some sort, might as well hit it head on. Standing quickly up which woke Jeb up from his slumber, I asked the sheriff, "Where can I find this capable woman?"

Sheriff Paulson slowly stood up before answering, "Her name is Tracy with no last name given and she has a room over at the Maysville Hotel, but take's her meals at the Mountain Man Saloon and spends the rest of her time there playing solitaire waiting on you."

Jeb and I had not eaten yet, so I decided the Mountain Man Saloon was a place to go grab some much-needed grub and find out what the mysterious and capable woman had to say, "Let's go Jeb and grab some chow and see if this woman is as beautiful as the sheriff thinks she is."

Jeb's dingo grin returned when I mentioned grub and he shot out the door as if they had set afire the jail house. Paulson laughed his hearty laugh as he watched Jeb streak out the door, "That is one fine mutt you got there, Patton."

Smiling as I turned to follow Jeb out the door, I said, "He is a character for sure."

Once on the boardwalk I fast palmed both of Schofield's one at a time and checked to see if I was fully loaded. Handsome woman or not, I was not walking into a saloon without being ready for anything that life threw my way. I was still a tad baffled on why this woman wanted to talk to me. Guess there is only one way to find out. Reaching the bottom of the wooden steps from the sheriff's office, I stopped and finished the cigar, inhaling deeply the smoky sweet aroma. Dropping the last of the cigar stub in the dirt, I put a boot to it to make sure it was out. Then Jeb and I started for the Mountain Man, leaving Cinders hitched in front of the sheriff's office.

Advancing through the bat-wing doors of the saloon, I saw the mysterious woman immediately. Paulson had not been exaggerating when he said she was a stunner. She sat alone at the table in the back of the saloon playing cards. I watched her for a few minutes before moving in her direction, letting my instincts try to ponder out what she was all about. Next to my departed wife, my eyes were telling me she might be the most beautiful woman I had ever seen. She had long blonde hair with piercing blue eyes. She had to be about 5'6" tall and dressed as a range hand in jeans, flannel shirt, dirty Stetson cattleman hat, and scuffed boots; none of which could hide her obviously womanly and alluring shape. In just the few moments of observation, this unknown woman had stirred my blood with her beauty, but I could also sense the danger that came with such a woman. So much in fact I almost walked out of the saloon thinking this might be trouble I did not need.

Walking cautiously across the saloon I stopped at her table and she looked up at me and her eyes narrowed a tad trying to figure out if I was a friend or foe. Deciding on which - a smile spread across her face, and then she spoke before I did, "You must be the famous bounty hunter Dale Lee Patton and his trusted dingo Jeb!"

CHAPTER 2

Feeling a tad distracted by her beauty which was somewhat alarming and I tried not to stare at this mysterious woman. Pointing at a chair across the table from her, I asked, "May I?"

The woman smiled again and quickly answered, "Of course Mr. Patton. My name is Tracy Marie Shaver, and I have been waiting nearly a week to talk to you."

Once I settled into the chair Jeb made a beeline for the chair right next to the woman and jumped up in it and promptly laid his head onto her arm. Jeb seemed to understand the discomfort this woman made me feel, and the dingo seemed to relish in it. Once he had his noggin plastered to the lady's arm he looked at me with that shit-eating grin of his. If Jeb had not been the best tracking dog I had ever known, I might have just shot him right there for showing off. Miss Shaver did what anyone would do when a friendly mutt attached themselves to you—she gave Jeb some loving. Still scratching Jeb behind his ears Miss Shaver said in a pleasant tone, "Your dingo seems to like me Mr. Patton."

Looking Jeb straight in the eye I stated in a matter-of-fact voice, "Well, Miss Shaver for 2 bits coin and buy me a beer you can have him."

Jeb raised his head and his shit-eating grin disappeared as he stared right back at me as Tracy Marie Shaver laughed out loud to the point that tears were starting to form in her eyes. Still chuckling, Miss Shaver said, "Jeb seems insulted, and he seemed to understand exactly what you said."

Turning my gaze from my dingo to Miss Shaver, "He is, and he does. Jeb is smarter than most folks I meet, which at times is a good thing, but most of the time he is just a pain in the behind. It would seem fate has made us partners and we are now stuck with each other. Jeb and I have not eaten yet, so whatever you need to say to us, just spit it out so Jeb and I can take our leave and grab us some grub."

Miss Shaver smile disappeared and had been replaced with a very serious face, but she continued to pet Jeb and she spoke again, "Please call me Tracy, and let me buy you and Jeb your supper for the night as I explain to you why I want to talk to you. I want to offer you both a job."

Once she said that she motioned the heavy-set and balding barkeep over and told him, "I would like to buy both gentlemen supper so whatever they want - just add it to my tab."

The barkeep ignored Jeb, which I found amusing since he was being such a show off tonight and looked at me and said in a very slow drawl, "Only thing on the spit tonight is turkey, and some fried taters and onions."

Nodding my head 'yes' and pointed at Jeb across the table, then I said, "That works for the both of us and please bring each of us some water, mine in a glass and the other gentleman's in a bowl."

Jeb's dingo smile returned when I called him a gentleman, which made Tracy and I both chuckle. As much as I hated it Tracy's easy laughter and her obvious affection towards Jeb was making this almost a pleasant encounter. It was only a minute, and the barkeep returned with our supper and as soon as he had placed our plates down. I quickly jumped up and walked around the table and moved Jeb's chair and his plate of taters and turkey about 4 feet away from Tracy. Tracy's face showed confusion by this maneuver. With Jeb still grinning, but now focused on the plate of food in front of him, I explained to Tracy, "It is best to be at least an arm's length away from Jeb when he starts to chow. As smart as he is; his table manners are for squat and messy. Embarrassing, really."

After I settled back in my chair I showed with a nod of my head towards Jeb and he dug in into his supper with obvious pleasure with his normal beastly manners. As I ate my supper, I kept my attention towards Tracy as she started to talk, "My now deceased great grandfather was a Frenchman named Astor Laurent. My grandfather was one of 4 French Canadians that had been trapping on the Snake River near Round Mountain. There was a territorial conflict with some American trappers, and by gunpoint the Americans stole their furs and traps of my grandfather's expedition and ran them off. My grandfather and the other 3 then traveled south along the headwaters of the Gunnison River, where they found a very large gold nugget the size of a chicken egg in the riverbed. Over the course of the next month, they successfully panned the gravel of the creek beds and accumulated a massive amount of gold. My great grandfather's expedition although successful in collecting this gold was ill-fated not only because they had the run in with the Americans but also the Ute Indians had discovered them while panning for their gold. My grandfather's expedition was attacked by the Ute's not for their gold, for it had no value to the Indians, but once again my grandfather was in someone else's territory. My grandfather and the others hastily packed their gold, and in the next ensuing 3 days there was a running battle with the Utes. One by one over those 3 days my grandfather's friends were killed and my grandfather had been wounded. Knowing there was no way that he could survive with moving so much gold with the Ute's still wanting his hair. He buried it. After making a detailed map of the location, he was able to escape and was the sole survivor of the expedition. Winter was fast closing in and my grandfather returned to Canada, hoping to raise enough capitol and men to go back and retrieve the gold the following spring. My grandfather never did recover from his wounds and before the following spring he developed an infection and passed away. The map he drew is now in my care. Mr. Patton, I have been told that you are a man with integrity and grit. I would like to hire Jeb and yourself to accompany me as I am now ready to retrieve this gold."

I had finished my meal as Tracy had told the tale of her great grandfather. It was an interesting tale of the Rocky Mountains, but not unfamiliar. Lost treasure tales were told at every campfire across these mountains every night. I realized by her telling of the tale that Tracy honestly believed she knew the location of the supposedly buried gold. My thought was the treasure tale was just a flight of fancy and probably the ramblings of an old man to his kin. I was even starting to feel guilty that I had accepted that she would pay for Jeb's and my meal, because there was no way in hell I was going to join her in this lost treasure tale folly. Though, I was curious on one thing. How was she planning on paying Jeb and me if we had taken her up on this opium pipe dream? Clearing my voice, before speaking, "I must be straight to the point. I am sure you believe this tale since someone had handed it down through your family. But stories such as this are told every night to wide-eyed children just before their bedtime. Not saying necessarily that it is not true, just saying it is more than likely it is just a fairy tale. I have one questions though. When you said—hire—how would you pay for Jeb's and my services?"

Tracy smile returned and her alluring blue eyes widen somewhat as she answered, "I like that question Mr. Patton. No doubt, you are a businessman. If I am correct, you just made $400 for one week of your time. I am willing to pay you $500 a week for 2 weeks of your and Jeb's valuable time for a grand total of $1000. I am also adding as a greater incentive of 10% of any gold that may be recovered to go along with the original $1000. I am also willing to give you that $1000 in advance."

The idea of making a $1000 for spending 2 weeks in the wilderness with a very handsome woman - most men would jump at that chance. It felt wrong to me to take that kind of money for what I was sure a fool's errand. There was one more question though I would like answered, "Tracy, I am a little confused, if you say you know where the gold is, how come you would need the likes of someone like Jeb and I to help you retrieve it?"

Tracy quit petting Jeb much to his displeasure, and she leaned onto the table with both forearms as her eyes narrowed as if she was trying to decide how much she wanted to tell me. After about a half-minute she cleared her voice and said, "As I stated early Mr. Patton, I have asked around and researched you with almost every law enforcement agency on the western slope that would return my telegraphs. I even spoke to the Pinkerton Detective Agency and every one of them told me you were not only trustworthy, but had integrity, which is an asset to this expedition. I was also that you are the most dangerous man to be reckoned with anywhere along the Rocky Mountain Frontier. And before you ask why I would need someone such as that - I will tell you. My Great Grandfather Astor Laurent gold is buried on Poncha Pass. I am sure you know that Poncha Pass is the territorial stronghold of Cadmel Sanderson. I do not need Jeb and you to help me find the gold and retrieve it. I need you both to keep me alive and out of the hands of Sanderson and his outlaws.

CHAPTER 3

Looking at this stunning blue-eyed blonde, I wish she had not told me she would ride into Cadmel Sanderson territory. For whatever reason, Sanderson had chosen the Poncha Pass as his hideout. Sanderson was a renegade Ute Indian that had a $1500 dead or alive bounty on his head. Over the last couple of years several bounty hunters had headed to Poncha pass to claim that bounty, but none had ever returned. Sanderson had left the reservation 3 years ago and now ran with a bunch of cutthroats that used to run with the Comancheros down south in Arizona and Mexico. Cadmel Sanderson had become their leader. To a man they were ruthless and had robbed, steal, butcher, rape, and killed anyone and everyone that they would run across. Sanderson's bunch had been linked to several massacre sites where the men had been slaughtered and mutilated. None of the woman from the sites had ever been found. It was rumored that once Cadmel and his men were done with the women, they would then sell them to the Comancheros in Mexico. A woman that looked like Tracy would fetch a handsome sum after being sold into slavery in the right place.

All women needed protection from those that meant them harm. Women such as Tracy and my departed wife Patricia also needed the protection they deserved from men such as myself. I had failed in providing that protection for my wife, and there was no way in hell was I going to let that happen again. I could not let this woman put herself into harm's way without me, even if I thought this treasure hunt was foolishness. Looking at my dingo Jeb as he squinted his eyes when he returned my gaze, and I knew that he would agree with my thoughts.

Leaning forward and placing both of my forearms on the table, I spoke, "Tracy Marie Shaver - you just hired the best bounty hunting and now treasure hunting duo on the Rocky Mountain frontier. Now I need to know where we are going. Where is grandfather's Laurent treasure map?"

A smile crossed Tracy's face as she looked to the bar and nodded towards a man there. The man was older and if I was to guess he was in his middle 50s. He was slender with wide shoulders of a prizefighter and wore a tied down Colt. His short hair under his cattleman creased cowboy was gray, and he wore a heavy and thick gray mustache. He approached the table and pulled up a chair on the other side of Jeb and sat down. Jeb immediately laid his head onto the strangers left arm. It would seem that Jeb just as I had sensed the goodness in this new stranger. Tracy wasted no time and introduced the man, "This is Ash Roundy. Ash has worked for my father for 30 years and now he works for me and is my most trusted advisor. Ash please show Mr. Patton grandfathers map"

Without hesitation Ash produced an ancient map from beneath his vest and laid it on top of the table and spun it so I could read it. After several minutes of studying the map, it impressed me. Considering at the time it was drawn, grandfather Laurent was being pursued by my very own ancestors, the Ute Indians. It was as Tracy mentioned - very detailed. So detailed in fact, I knew the exact area of the supposedly buried treasure.

The treasure site marked by the common "X" marks the spot was at the confluence of 2 small creeks, the San Luis and Dorsey. Both creeks headwaters began at the base of Methodist Mountain.

This meeting of the waters of the San Luis and Dorsey was just over a day's ride from Maysville. The good news would be this area was on the northern edge of the territory that we knew Sanderson and his gang like to roam. There was a good possibility we could get in and out without him ever knowing we were there.

Tracy and Ash were both looking over my shoulders as I studied the map. And Tracy pointed to a note that her grandfather had scribbled on the map, then circled it, and said, "That note is the big mystery. I have had several professional map makers look at this note and nobody can tell me what it means. To the best of my family's knowledge, my grandfather did not know anyone named Johnnie or Karin."

I almost laughed out loud when Tracy said it was a big mystery. For it was that note that almost had me believing there might be some truth to this treasure tale. Looking at Tracy I said, "That note makes this entire tale more believable to me than anything else you told me or showed me. Johnnie and Karin are not people, but a place. A very specific place."

Tracy and Ash both looked confused then Tracy laughed when she said with a smile, "I see contacting you Mr. Patton was the best thing I have done in this quest by far. Explain to us how and why that note is so important."

Touching the note on the map I enlightened my new employer, "It is my belief the word Karin had been misspelled by your grandfather and he meant 'cairn' as in rock cairn. The name Johnnie I also understand as being a - Stone Johnnie. Stone Johnnie and a rock cairn are the same thing, just a different name. I believe you grandfather marked the treasure with a Stone Johnnie. Throughout the west they have been called by many names such as Rock Johnnies, Johnny Rocks, stone men, butte markers, water markers, and more recently in the Dakota territories they have been called sheepherders monuments. They are markers that are used to find something quickly. First used by Indians to mark waterholes, early settlers quickly adopted this way of marking a location, Stone Johnnies were built by piling flat rocks on top of each other to make a skinny pyramid or column. The Johnnie or Cairn on your grandfather's map is the exact location your grandfather buried his gold. The significant news is that a Stone Johnnie unless disturbed by someone will stand the test of time down through the years. Meaning if it was built, more than likely it is still there."

You could see the sense of relief spread over Tracy's face, as if someone now believed the treasure tale of her grandfather. In the growing excitement of the moment, she spun me and fell into my arms, giving me a hug. It took me by surprise and she held me for what seemed a long time and when we slowly parted I could see in her eyes; she enjoyed it as much as I did. Having her heart beating next to mine felt good, maybe too good. There was no doubt this woman stirred my blood.

The next morning Tracy purchased enough supplies for the 2 week expedition. Tracy also purchased 5 pack horses. Not for the supplies, but to carry the gold out once it was located. She believed in her heart that the treasure tale was true and had confidence we would find it. I admired her for her determination. She was one hell of a woman.

With our roles established, Tracy was the boss and the driving force behind the expedition. Ash would be the horse wrangler and biscuit shooter for meals. Jeb and I would be the scouts and provide security for all as we moved out at noon towards Poncha Pass.

It was 2nd day at midday after leaving Maysville is when I pulled back on Cinder's reins and brought her to a standstill on a mountainside overlooking San Luis and Dorsey creeks below. Using my binoculars I surveyed the confluence of the 2 small creeks and even from this distance I saw it. Just like the map said there would be—I saw a 6 foot tall Stone Johnnie standing tall and straight like a beacon in the afternoon sun.

Tracy had ridden up beside me and was close enough that our legs were touching. Handing her the binoculars, I pointed towards the Stone Johnnie. After a minute of looking Tracy lowered the field glasses and said, "Dale, are we close yet?"

With a smile I quickly said, "Look once more and tell me what you see."

Tracy did as I asked and after a full minute said, "I see 2 small creeks flowing into each other and a pile of rocks on one side of where they flow together."

Still smiling, I asked, "Do you think that pile of rocks is something that nature would do?"

Several more seconds passed before Tracy lowered the field glasses and a smile broadened on her face as she looked at me. Her eyes widen with excitement and said, "That is the Stone Johnnie you were talking about. That is where my grandfather's gold is!"

Having said that and in the moment's enthusiasm, Tracy leaned over and kissed me. Not a small kiss, but a kiss like lovers would share. Once again taken by surprise and I almost didn't kiss her back. We separated and looked at each other for a spell until Jeb broke the trance we were both in and barked twice. Looking at my Dingo who was sitting on his butt watching us with a tilted head as if he was trying to decide what Tracy and I were doing. He looked so comical at that moment Tracy and I both laughed. Turning my attention to the task at hand, I told Tracy, "Let's go find some gold!"

CHAPTER 4

Before moving down into the possible treasure site, I quick palmed both of my pistols and added a sixth round into the bean wheel to be fully loaded. We would probably be here for several days and I wanted to be ready in case Cadmel Sanderson and his cutthroats were out and about.

After an hour of moving through the thick stand of evergreen and aspens trees, we crossed Dorsey Creek. With more excitement than I would care to admit, Tracy and I quickly dismounted as we moved closer to the stone Johnnie. Tracy was so enthusiastic while touching the monument, she quickly ran behind it and fell into a hole in the ground.

After hearing the thud as she landed and her gasp for air, I moved around the monument and jumped down into the grave like hole to see if she was okay. Reaching down to help her into a sitting position and in a concerned voice, "Tracy, are you okay? Do you think you sprained or broke anything?"

Tracy had a pained expression on her face, but could move her arms and legs and seemed to be no worse for wear. That is when she started laughing and said, "No Dale, it seems everything is still working, but my pride has been damaged somewhat. That was a foolish thing for me to do."

Once I was sure Tracy was physically okay, I studied the depression she had fallen into. Over the years this hole had silted in some from the rains and the snows, but I realized it had been a dug-out hole. This hole was nothing in nature had created, it had been dug by men with shovels. Helping Tracy so she was now standing, I could see now she had been sitting on some remnants of coarsely woven cloth. Reaching down, I picked it up and study it closer and I found it to be a handful of decaying burlap. Like a burlap sack that you would use to haul something in—something, maybe, like gold ore?

Climbing out of the hole, I reached down and helped Tracy out. Ash and Jeb had joined us on the rim of the excavated hole and Ash said it before I could, "I wonder who in the hell dug that hole?"

As soon as Ash asked that question I could see the excitement of the day fade from Tracy's face as it was dawning on all of us at the same time that someone had probably already found the gold and it was long gone.

Not to say we would not explore the possibility of the treasure was still being here. We set up camp right at the junction of the 2 creeks. I was not happy with the site. We had water, and the trees kept the wind at bay most of the time, but it was a campsite that would be hard to defend if needed.

The first day Tracy and Ash went to work with the shovels and picks we had brought to dismantle the stone Johnnie to dig directly below it. Jeb pitched in, digging with his paws, and seemed to enjoy the company of Tracy and Ash. Knowing we were in Sanderson range and stronghold I thought it best to come up with a plan of retreat to a defensible place to make a stand if needed.

Following along Dorsey Creek, Cinders and I zigged and zagged through the aspens and evergreens in an easterly direction back towards Methodist Mountain. We followed the creek until it sputtered out and became a bubbling brook that seeped from the mountain. The location was just what I was looking for. Within several feet of the beginnings of Dorsey Creek was a cave. A cave big enough that could house several horses and all of us at the same time. Above the cave was a sheer cliff of at least 200 feet or more, and I could think of no one that would be foolhardy enough to take us by surprise by climbing down the face of that rock wall. In front of the cave we had at least 30 yards of clearing that could be easily defended if needed. There was water seeping from the mountain close, and all we would need firewood and food for an extended stay. I spent the rest of the day stocking it with down firewood for a long stay if we were under siege.

Returning to camp that evening, I found supper ready, but Tracy and Ash looked worn and beat. They had worked hard dismantling the stone Johnnie and had dug several feet below to no avail. The only one that was chipper was Jeb—who seemed to be having the time of his life on this adventure.

After supper I told Tracy and Ash what I had found in ways of being able to retreat if needed and we all agreed that I would take one packhorse with a week of our food supplies and take it to the cave. We could retrieve all supplies if required or when we had exhausted our search for the gold and were ready to head back to Maysville.

It was on the third day when we were all digging and using the pickax I noticed something move across the skyline to the west about midday. Using my binoculars I discovered it was not just something, but a man on a horse and he was studying us with his own set of field glasses. It could be anyone, but giving the territory we were in, I didn't like it at all. Putting my binoculars away, I said in a matter-of-fact voice, "Jeb, time to hunt!"

Explaining to Tracy and Ash we were being observed and to simply keep doing what they were doing. Once in the saddle I gave Jeb the nod in the direction I wanted him to go. Once Jeb started using his nose to move out, Cinder's and I followed him. It was time to find out who the stranger was.

As Jeb and I moved closer to the man on the rise, he acted like he had not even seen me move out towards him. Each time I could glimpse him in between the leaves and the tree trunks, he was still watching Ash and Tracy with his field glasses. It would be my guess that the lone rider was focused in on Tracy and he was watching her every move. That was good news since I could move in on him without him knowing it, but bad news when it probably came to his intentions.

Knowing now the rider had no clue I was moving towards him, I even moved further to the north of him so I could come up on him from his side. The tree line I was using for cover ended 20 yards away from the rider who was still intent on watching Tracy as she moved about. Now seeing him this up close, I could tell he was Hispanic and Indian mix with 2 long dark braids that reached to the middle of his back. He was not dressed as an Indian would dress; he was dressed as a bandit or Comanchero would dress in filthy buckskins with a sombrero hanging by a rawhide string from his neck to his back. He had a pistol tied down to his right leg and a fringed knife sheaf hanging off his belt. Moving out into the clearing he was still so focused on watching Tracy he still did not see me. Tracy was a stunner in any man's language.

Dismounting quietly, I nodded towards Jeb and he sprang into action and went straight for the lone rider. The horse was just as surprised and startled as the rider was when Jeb suddenly appeared out of seemingly nowhere. The horse bucked violently 3 times and tossed the rider to the ground, where he landed face first on his field glasses. The horse wanting no more of Jeb bolted off and down the side of the hill, heading south. Watching the horse out of the corner of my eye, I saw the now rider less horse heading towards another rider about a mile in the distance. My first thought was "Shit!"

The man on the ground gained some of his senses and tried to roll to his side and reached for his pistol in his holster, which I kicked not so gently out of his hand. Pointing my right-handed Schofield 45 right at his head, I asked, "Who are you? And why are you watching us?"

The rider that was a mile in the distance saw the rider less horse and started at a fast trot in my direction. By me not noticing the 2nd rider to begin with - this was now going to get ugly.

The dirty buckskin fellow on the ground did not reply and looked pissed. I am going to ask you one more time before your buddy gets here, "Who are you? And why are you watching us?"

This time he replied furiously and in Spanish, "Ambos viajamos con Cadmel Sanderson. Y ahora eres un muerto viviente."

I didn't speak Spanish, but his tone and using Cadmel Sanderson was enough for me to realize this whole expedition just got dangerous, really dangerous.

The man who was riding towards us suddenly pulled back hard on his horse's reins when he noticed me and that I had his compadre on the ground. He spun his horse and started in the opposite direction, abandoning his buddy. He was still 250 yards away. Telling Jeb loudly "WATCH" I ran towards Cinders. Jeb immediately took over watching the character on the ground and snapped at him each time he moved. I knew Jeb would keep him under control. Reaching Cinders, I pulled my 50 caliber Sharps that I owned and then laid it over the saddle on Cinders and took aim at the fleeing man. By the time I lined him up in the sights and adjusted for the arc of the bullet, he was 500 yards out. If I hit him, it would be a miracle at that distance. I gently squeezed the trigger. The bullet seemed to take forever, but it found the target. The man slumped in the saddle, then immediately set back up. I must have just grazed him, because a 50 caliber slug full body would have dropped him from the saddle. That didn't happen.

Cursing my luck, I shoved the 50 sharps back into its scabbard and returned to the one that had gotten bucked off. Once I was close Jeb backed off and stood by my side. The man then gained his feet and stood up before me and in a heightened voice said, "¡Eres un gringo muerto! Cadmel te cortará la garganta. ¡Demonios, te voy a matar yo mismo!"

Having said his piece, he reached under his shirt for a belly gun. One that during the rush of excitement with the other rider I did not look for. The bandit was slow, too slow, and I palmed my right-handed Schofield and fired twice—center chest - killing him before he slumped to the ground.

Leaving the bandit where he had fallen, because critters needed to eat too, I quickly mounted Cinder's and swung her around and trotted her back towards our camp. This situation had gotten out of hand and we needed to leave before Sanderson's man that had gotten away brought some more of his friends back here.

Once Jeb and I reached the campsite, I dismounted rapidly and started barking orders about packing up and leaving. I laid it out to Tracy and Ash what had happened with the killing of the bandit and the one that got away and that we needed to head back to Maysville pronto.

Tracy and Ash looked concerned, but did not move. Tracy looked me square in the eye and said, "I can't go just yet."

That threw me for a loop and I said with more than enough concern for everyone here, "What the hell do you mean? I can't go just yet."

Tracy raised her arms nervously and motioned to Ash to step forward when she said, "Ash, show Dale what we found. Show him the gold we uncovered right after he left."

Ash stepped forward and handed me the largest gold nugget I had ever seen. It was about the size of a small chicken egg. As I was gauging the weight of the nugget in my hand Tracy said, "We found another burlap sack and we think there is more below it. That is why I can't go."

Handing the nugget back to Ash, I said, "I don't think you understand the seriousness of our situation now. I killed one and wounded another one of Sanderson's gang. Even if the one I wounded dies before he makes their camp. They will look for them and they will find us. And they will want blood!"

Tracy looked bewildered for a second, then quickly recovered and stated, "I get that Dale. This gold, this quest is everything I have ever dreamed of since my grandfather told me the tale of his adventure. This is my grandfather's legacy and I and not leaving until I have recovered what's left."

Almost in disbelief and I said in a very stern tone, "Even if it gets us all killed?"

Tracy countered with, "No, I do not expect Ash, Jeb, or yourself to stay. But I am staying Dale. I have to do this!"

Ash stepped forward again and stood next to Tracy and had his say, "If Tracy is staying, so am I."

Jeb crossed the space in between Tracy and me, then turned facing me and planted his butt nearly on her left foot and barked once, giving me the stink eye. Jeez, I had a full-blown rebellion and mutiny. Throwing my hands up in defeat I blurted out, "If we all are going to get killed, Show me what we are dying for."

What Tracy and Ash showed me was what dreams were made of. They had unearthed another rotted burlap sack full of gold. And it appeared to be at least another below it. I had to admit it - just the thought of finding such a treasure was exciting. That still did not lessen the fact that we all were now in grave danger. Looking at all 3, I said in a matter-of-fact voice, "Since we all are staying - all 3 of you will do it my way. If I say—'jump'—you ask, 'how high?' If I say—'we are moving out'—you say, 'how fast?' We sleep in alternating 4 hour shifts. I will catch some shut-eye first, as you both dig. As soon as you recover gold, it needs to be stowed away on a packhorse immediately. After I wake up Jeb and I will post up on the trail and watch for Sanderson and his bunch and try to slow them down a tad. At that point you both switch back and forth between sleeping and digging so someone is always recovering the gold. That's the deal!"

Tracy flew into my arms and kissed me with all she had. The kiss once again surprised me, and I almost did not return it. Slowly she pulled away, and we both were flush with the passion of the moment and I was for a loss of words, when Tracy broke the trance and said, "Ash and I better get to digging and you need to get some sleep."

As I laid down to get some shut-eye I could not help but wonder if by agreeing to stay that it had doomed all of us.

CHAPTER 5

On watch, the night passed slowly as my thoughts were a rambling mess. I was questioning if I had made the right decision to stay and let Tracy recover what was left of her grandfather's gold. I kept telling myself she was going to stay regardless, but I knew in my heart that was not true. If I had been more forceful in deciding to leave and return later, she would have gone along with that. She would have had no choice. If Ash and Tracy were killed, because I made the wrong decision it would haunt me forever. Running it through my thinker repeatedly, it all came down to, I just could not tell Tracy—no. The blonde headed stunner was tugging at my heartstrings and the conflict I was having was - I wanted her. The guilt for finally admitting that my feelings had run the gauntlet for Tracy was spinning my heart and mind out of control. I loved my wife Patricia like no other, and in her death I found no peaceful resolution or retribution. Was it possible for me to still love Patricia and want to explore loving another? Jeb was having no issues, for he was sound asleep laying in my lap. It would seem that Jeb was just that much smarter than me.

The dawn of the new day was here as the sun was trying to rise in the east. The air was fresh and the slight breeze from the north brought the tingling smell of evergreen. My gut instinct was telling me - it would not be thoughts of love that let us all survive this day. To survive it was going to take the coldness of lead and the smell of burnt gunpowder to survive what was coming. Pushing the thoughts of Tracy to the back of my mind, I brought forth the killer instinct that lived in my soul.

The new day was now raining down sunlight on the Rocky Mountains. The early morning mountain mist was slowly fading as the sun moved across the trees. Using my binoculars, I focused on the trail south of my position. At first I thought it was just a shadow that was growing shorter as the sun rose higher in the sky. It was not long before I realized the shadow I had been watching was a man on horseback moving in my direction. Not just one man - in the next several minutes more men on horseback appeared on the trail. Watching and counting it took a full 30 minutes before I was confident I was looking at all the men on the trail. No packhorse, no wagons, 12 men riding in single file. The 2nd man in line slouched in his saddle as if he was sleeping or possibly wounded. Could this be the man I tagged with the 50 Caliber Sharps?

Picking up the 50 caliber Sharps as I was loading it, I then laid out two extra shells next to it for fast loading. If this was Cadmel Sanderson and his bandits, I was hoping to even the odds some before they even got close. As they moved closer, I could now make out their features and the 2nd man in line was having a tough time staying in the saddle. The one leading I did not believe was Cadmel Sanderson, for he seemed to have the features of Mexican and not that of an Indian. They were all dressed similar and in the manner of the Comancheros. Sombreros, and dirty buckskins, and each to a man had at least one fully loaded bandolier crossing their chests. These men on the trail south of me were not trappers, miners, cowhands, or merchants. There was no question in my mind that these men were bandits and part of the Cadmel Sanderson gang. Studying the riders more, I decided the last man in line looked like a full blood Indian and was probably Sanderson. That was smart. He had no idea what they were riding into and offered his men as targets in front. Cold-hearted, but smart.

At 300 yards I tried to get a bead on the last rider, but the men in front were blocking him and never gave me a shot. Deciding now was not the time to be picky, I lined up on the first man in line, took a deep breath, and slowly squeezed the trigger. Even at this distance, the 50 caliber punched the man out of the saddle. The rest of the riders momentarily froze before they started to scatter, which gave me just enough time to reload and fire again. Punching the third man in line from his saddle with a 50 caliber slug as he tried to reach the safety of the evergreen trees. By the time I reloaded, all the remaining bandits had reached the cover of the trees except the 2nd man in line, the one I had wounded the day earlier. He was still on the trail, slouched in his saddle. Wounded and out of the fight, I let him live.

Not counting the wounded man, the remaining 9 riders had reached the evergreens on both sides of the trail. I could see the movement of the horse's legs and the shadows of the men as they scurried about trying to regain control of their mounts. Taking a bead on a shadow on the west side of the trail, I squeezed off another shot. A miss. Time to move out and retreat to Ash and Tracy.

Even before I could stand to make my withdrawal those that hid in the evergreens started firing on my position. Keeping low I took one last look with the field binoculars and I could see the remaining unwounded Sanderson 9 moving briskly using the evergreens as cover towards my position, firing randomly in my direction.

Still staying low, I grabbed Cinder's reins and pulled her backwards to a point I felt was safe enough to mount. Once in the saddle I reined her around hard as I spoke to Jeb, "Let's make tracks out of here Jeb!"

Reaching the treasure site, Ash and Tracy were busy gathering all the packhorses. I was hoping they would have been ready to pull out before I got here. Dismounting, I pitched in, gathering the horses. Tracy's horse Carolina, Ash's horse Sadie, and my horse Cinders were calm. The remaining pack horses Wisteria, Cherish, Rosette, Midsummer and Amethyst were skittish and went to bucking because of the Sanderson outlaws unrelenting gunfire on my last known position, not knowing I had already fled down the mountainside. This was taking too long. Looking at Tracy and in a hurried voice, "How many packhorses are carrying the gold?"

Tracy was sweating and working feverishly trying to bring the horses under control answered me in an alarmed voice, "Only Wisteria! She has about 200 pounds of gold packed on her!"

Making the only decision I could, and the fact there were 9 furious men riding down hard on us. In a raised voice so everyone could hear me, "Cut all the horses loose except Wisteria! Do it now!"

Ash, Tracy, and I went to work cutting all the packhorses loose except Wisteria. Keeping my eyes on the mountain, I saw Sanderson's riders break the skyline, and they straightaway began firing down on our position. Just as I palmed my left-handed Scofield a bullet fired from my right singed my cheek. Shit! They had already breached the clearing we were in! Spinning to the right to face the new threat, I heard Tracy's Colt army revolver fire twice in quick succession. Tracy had shot the man shooting at me. A quick glance of acknowledgment I return my attention to those on the hill and unloaded my revolver in their direction, hoping to slow them down as they advanced on us.

We were successful in cutting the panicky horses loose. With all of us now mounted I pointed to Ash who had the reins of Wisteria and the gold I yelled, "Go! Head to the cave!"

Ash was first, then Tracy as they spurred their horses into a gallop. Jeb and I stood our ground for another minute, providing cover fire for their retreat. Pulling my Winchester, I started levering shots toward the bandits. The last shell before emptying the Winchester struck home as I dropped another bandit.

My Winchester and now one of my Scofield's were empty, with no time to reload. Reining Cinders around Jeb and I followed Tracy and Ash as we all moved towards the headwaters of Dorsey Creek and the cave at the base of Methodist Mountain.

Pushing Cinders hard, we zigged and zagged through the evergreens and aspen trees, hoping to not to get too close to have a branch separate me from the saddle. Since Jeb was smaller and did not have to worry about tree branches, he was far away in front of me; he had already deciphered out where we were heading.

Looking ahead, I could catch glimpses of Ash, Tracy, and Wisteria as they weaved and maneuvered through the trees. I had not slowed the bandits down much as much as I had hoped for. Now they were close behind and taking potshots at me as we all raced through the trees. Every few moments I could hear the angry whine of a bullet that had passed too close for comfort.

Tracy and Ash had reached the entrance to the cave and had already dismounted and stashed their horses inside the entrance when I broke into the clearing, riding hell bent on Cinders. They set up with their Winchesters and were aiming them in my direction or hopefully behind me. Just as I was half-way across the clearing and ready to dismount I felt the slap first then the blistering heat as a bullet tore into my lower right side. Trying to dismount Cinders on the run failed as I fell to the ground hard. Not hard enough that I blacked out. Somewhat dazed, but with enough wits about me, I saw Tracy and Ash advance while under fire from the cave to where I had fallen firing their Winchesters. Ash helped me up and moved me quickly back towards the cave as Tracy covered us with return fire as she retreated.

Cinders and Jeb were still outside the cave and I yelled at them both, "Cinders and Jeb get your butt's inside here!"

Following my voice and shouted directions, Cinders and Jeb both moved swiftly into the safety of the cave.

Silence enveloped the mountain as all gunfire stopped. My wound was a through and through in the meaty part of my right side above the hip. No bone or vitals had been hit. Tracy stopped the bleeding in short order. It hurt like hell, but I had worse and would survive this.

After getting patched up we made sure we were all reloaded, one thing we were not short of was ammo. Looking at Tracy and Ash's faces, I could see the determination of them both. There was no give up in either of them and if today was the day that death took me—I had pride to be with those that I had fighting next to me on this day. Both of them had shown courage and strength today.

Ash had positioned himself at the entrance and as soon as I joined him the Sanderson gang opened up with everything they had. Bullets were flying every which way and several had ricocheted around on the inside of the cave. One ricochet came so close to Wisteria that she started bucking and in a madden frenzy bolted for the entrance.

Ash and I had our heads down trying not to get shot when Wisteria hot-footed by us carrying all the gold. Ash reacted without thinking, took off after her.

Using my Winchester to provide covering fire was almost useless since I had not had enough time to pinpoint the bandits outside the cave. I was firing swiftly, but randomly, with no actual targets. Tracy straightaway took the spot that Ash had just vacated, and she fired into the tree line as blindly as I was.

Ash was able to reach Wisteria and grab her reins and she once again went to bucking. As Ash was trying to bring her under control a bandit on horseback broke into the clearing and leveled his pistol at Ash. Ash spun his Winchester at the newest threat and both of them fired at the same time. Both the bandit and Ash's bullets hit home. Ash went down hard and the bandit dropped from his horse with Ash's bullet in his chest and was dead before he hit the ground.

Doing the math in my head, I reckoned there were 6 bandits left, and they had not let up on the barrage of gunfire. I saw a large shadow move in the tree line and I shot it and the shadow dropped. Even with the constant fusillade of gunfire, I had heard a man yell out when my bullet found him.

As Tracy reloaded, she noticed Ash was moving, "Dale! Ash is still alive!"

Tracy lifted her Winchester to her shoulder and firing as she rushed out of the cave towards Ash before I could stop her. It was official - I had lost control of this gunfight. Cursing as I stood - both Jeb and I followed Tracy out of the cave into the clearing providing cover fire.

One bandit appeared suddenly out of the tree line, heading for Tracy. Tracy saw him and brought her Winchester in line with him and squeezed the trigger—to no avail. Her Winchester was empty.

Before the bandit could capture Tracy I fired and caught him in the throat, dropping him firmly to the ground. Another appeared on horseback heading for Tracy, and I shot him out of the saddle just as he broke the tree line.

My sole purpose of trying to protect Tracy from the 2 bandits on horseback, I had neglected my back, and I felt the cold steel of a pistol barrel as it was punched into the back of my head. One of the remaining bandits had gotten behind and now had the drop on me. In an icy voice the bandit said, "Drop the rifle! And raise your hands!"

Looking at Tracy I saw fear cross her face for the first time today and as I dropped my Winchester, the realization sank in that I had once again failed a woman that I cared for. The last remaining 2 bandits appeared from the tree line and walked up to Tracy. The taller one violently grabbed her hair and slapped her to the ground. Jeb went for the bandit with his hackles raised, and the bandit kicked Jeb so hard in the head that my dingo flew 6 feet in the air backwards before landing with a thud. Jeb was dead or knocked out, because he laid motionless on the ground. Given the chance, that bandit had just signed his own death warrant for slapping Tracy and kicking my dog. The man with the pistol to my head yelled at the man who had slapped Tracy and had kicked my dog, "You hit the woman again Mace, I will kill you. She is too valuable to be beaten!"

Shoving the barrel harder into the back of my noggin, the man behind me said in an almost curious voice, "Now who the hell are you, mister? Have your come to collect the bounty on my head? If so, I want your name so I can carve it on my kitchen table with the others that have tried."

With my hands still raised and slowly turning around so I could see the man that had me at a disadvantage as he continued to point his cocked pistol now at my face. He was full blood Indian with the high cheekbones of the Utes. From the renderings on wanted posters I had seen, there was no doubt this was Cadmel Sanderson, the renegade Ute. The other thing I was sure of was that Sanderson had no idea the packhorse now grazing contently nearby was carrying nearly 200 pounds of gold. Sanderson study me and questioned, "You're an Indian? Now what is your name?"

With not one ounce of fear in my voice, "I am half Ute Indian and half Scottish. My name is Dale Lee Patton. And—no—we did not come here for the bounty on your head. Sanderson, you lost most of your men for nothing. If your men had left us alone, they all would still be alive."

Sanderson's eyes narrowed, and he quickly said, "I think you lie Dale Lee Patton. I have heard of you and some say you are the most feared bounty hunter of the Rocky Mountains. You came to kill me for blood money!"

Tracy had scooted on the ground towards Ash and held his head, trying to comfort our wounded friend. I almost laughed when I spoke again, "You got a swelled head there Cadmel thinking this is all about you and a paltry bounty. We came for the almost 200 pounds of gold on that pack horse over yonder."

Sanderson's eyes widen when I mentioned the gold. He motioned with a shake of his head for Mace and the other bandit over to Wisteria. Both men seemed a tad confused, but meandered towards the packhorse, leaving Tracy and Ash unarmed, but alone. I reckoned this was the only time I would ever again have the last remaining 3 bandits, including Sanderson, in front of me. I just had to wait for it.

Mace and the other now were fully focused on Wisteria and the possibility of the gold.

Sanderson's eyes were still on me. Mace holstered his pistol and pulled an 8 inch blade knife from under his shirt and cut the pack straps. Both packs dropped heavily to the ground and split open, spilling Tracy's grandfather's gold out on to the ground for all to see.

The sudden appearance of so much gold distracted Sanderson's as he looked longingly at the gold. This gave the momentary advantage I was needing.

Dropping my left arm with all the strength I had on to Sanderson's pistol arm to avert it away from me, then following up with a right-hand punch to his face. Sanderson instinctively fired, but harmlessly into the ground far to my left. As he stumbled backwards trying not to fall I quick palmed both of my Scofield's using the right-handed one I fired at both bandits that were standing next to the gold and Wisteria. My first shot caught the shorter one just above where his belt buckle would have been if he had been wearing one. My 2nd shot slammed home into the center chest of Mace, the man that had slapped Tracy and kicked Jeb. My 3rd shot from my right pistol punched a hole through Mace's face just above his nose, killing him before he dropped. My left-handed Scofield was for Sanderson and I fired 3 shots from it in such quick a manner that they almost sounded as one. Cadmel

Sanderson the renegade Ute was now dead with 3 closely placed rounds placed not an inch apart from each other in his center chest.

Now that all 3 remaining outlaws were down and out, I spun towards Jeb as I holstered both of my pistols. Looking to Tracy as I reached Jeb and said, "Tracy, how is Ash?"

As Tracy was tearing her shirt to make a bandage to stuff in the bullet hole to stem the bleeding she said, "It is bad Dale, if I can stop the bleeding, he might have a chance!"

Dropping to my knees next to Jeb, I feared the worse. Gently touching his face, the dingo's eyes fluttered and finally opened. He was dazed, but very much alive! Breathing deeply, I picked Jeb up gently and rolled him into my chest as I turned slightly to sit on my end gate holding the dingo looking in his face. Jeb's shit-eating grin appeared, and I knew at that moment he was going to be okay. Almost with a laugh I said to my partner, "I knew you had a thick skull, but until today buddy I did not understand how thick."

CHAPTER 6

A week after returning to Maysville, Jeb and I saw Tracy to the train as she headed back home to Canada to secure her grandfather's legacy. Whatever that meant. There was no kiss goodbye, just a long hug and promises from both of us to stay in touch. It was as if the kiss and the intense feelings we had shared on the mountain had never existed. Maybe there had been too much bloodshed or maybe it was Tracy felt my hesitation, because I still loved my wife. As we watched the train fade into the morning sun, I knew I would miss the stunning and capable woman, but realized this was more than likely the last time I would ever see her.

Ash was still bedridden from his wound, but was expected to make a full recovery before he could rejoin his employer in Canada. Tracy had been generous to Ash and had given him 10% of the 238 pounds of her grandfather's gold that had been recovered.

Jeb and I also had our biggest payday to date. We received the $1000 wages, $1500 bounty on Sanderson, besides 10% of all the gold recovered.

When Jeb and I could no longer see the smoke from the eastbound train I sat down on the boardwalk at the train depot with my legs dangling over the edge. Jeb cuddle up to me and laid his head in my lap and seemed just as sad as I that Tracy had gone back home. Scratching behind Jeb's right ear the way he liked it, I said in a calming voice to him, "Well my friend, we got a sizable sum in the bank and maybe we should just wander the timberline for a spell."

A red-tail hawk took pity on us and flew 3 ever-widening circles over our heads, making the kuk-kuk-kuk call that they do. With pleasure, I watched the hawk for a long time. Then with one last glance and full circle overhead the hawk decided he had some place to be, and he headed due west back into the mountain wilderness. That was enough of a sign to me. Still tussling Jeb's ears, I told him, "Jeb, it would seem our mountains are calling. Time to go home."

PATTON
BOUNTY
HUNTER
6th
Adventure

CHAPTER 1

The 16 days and 350 hundred mile trail to Keota, Colorado had been cold, muddy, and miserable. Late autumn was not the ideal time to be traveling so far from Jeb my cinnamon-colored short-haired Australian born dingo, Cinders my blood bay three-year-old mare's, and my normal range of the west slope of the Rocky Mountains to the flatlands in northeast Colorado.

Keota was a settlement in the grasslands of Pawnee Butte. Keota was an Indian name meaning "gone for a visit" or some said it meant "the fire goes out." Keota was a brand new railroad train stop on the Old Prairie Dog Express of the Colorado-Wyoming division of the Burlington-Missouri railroad.

I had gotten a telegram asking for my help in Montrose from a lifelong friend of mine, Oscar Polichio. The telegram was short and tragic for his 14-year-old daughter Annie had been kidnapped, savaged, and strangled by a man named Tom Foster. Oscar was my best friend growing up and had saved my life from drowning when

I was 7 years old. I had been young and stupid and had gotten caught up in some rapids while swimming in the South Platte River, and Oscar risked his own life to save mine. Pretty brave thing for a 7-year-old. Something like that sticks with a man his entire life, and I had never forgotten it. Owing Oscar my life, he had asked nothing of me until this tragic event. If he needed my help—all he had to do was ask. Sending a quick reply telling my friend I was on my way. Jeb and I bought supplies for the long trip and made our way out of the mountains and headed for the settlement of Keota.

Oscar had married and had 2 sons and 1 daughter and had homesteaded 3 miles east of Keota. The child killer Tom Foster was the man that Oscar had friended and had put the 20-year-old man to work on his farm. As it turned out Foster was not the man Oscar thought him to be.

Oscar fired Foster after he cornered Annie and had tried to force himself on her. Oscar had severely beat the man and sent him packing, fighting the urge to kill him. The next morning Annie's mother had found her dead after she had gone to hay the mules and horses. Annie had fought her killer and during the death struggle she had grabbed the one and only clue that made Foster the killer. In her clutched hand was a bandana with Indian beads sewn into it. The one of a kind bandana was always in Foster's vest pocket. Foster of course was nowhere to be found, for he had fled the area after he had murdered Annie.

Oscar's woodcraft and tracking skills were not on par with mine—he had searched in vain for Foster, before losing his trail. Oscar distraught with guilt and frustration and knowing of the tremendous debt I owed him, he sent the telegram. I was happy to oblige my lifelong friend.

The day I reached Keota, the local law had received news that a young man with scratches still healing and matching Foster's description had been seen in Stoneham, Colorado.

Stoneham was 28 miles east of Keota and was a settlement some Belgium immigrants had established. The long and short of it was that after 2 days of late autumn travel Oscar, Jeb, and I caught up with Annie's killer. A father's justice was swiftly served, and Foster drew his last breath after confessing to his deadly deed.

After the death of the man that had brought so much misery to my lifelong friend, I spent the following 2 days with my friend Oscar and his family. It was not long before Jeb, Cinders, and I felt the calling of the mountains in the far western horizon. Knowing it was late in the autumn, we were more than prepared for the coming of the snow from old man winter. After a long hug with my friend, we headed west; we headed home.

It was the 3rd morning after leaving Keota, and northeast of Fort Vasquez it started to snow. Jeb and I had watched the storm blowing in from the north the day before and last night it settle in overhead, blocking out the stars and the moon. The northern air was crisp, cold, and below freezing as my breath froze on my mustache and beard. Jeb so far seems to be okay, but I worried about him since the winter coat of an Australian dingo didn't seem like much against the icy winds of Colorado. Jeb was tougher than most dogs and had wintered fine in Colorado before. Although I worried about him I knew he would let me know if the cold was getting the best of him. Cinders my horse was born and raised above timberline and the cold weather seemed to have no effect on her.

By mid-morning the snow and the wind increased, blowing north to south. I had been looking for some shelter to ride out the storm since early morning to no avail. There was not one tree to be seen in all the countryside surrounding me, this country was desolate and empty except for snow and wind. This was one of those storms that could get dangerous in short order, and my gut instinct was telling me this was one of those times. We were moving in a southwest direction as the snowstorm blossomed into a full-blown Colorado plains blizzard at midday. The snow and blistering wind now was creating 1 foot drifts and Jeb was struggling to walk in it. Dismounting and gathering up Jeb in my arms, I then put the dingo in front of my saddle horn to let him ride double with me. My fingers had numbed to the point I had to dig out my old wolf's fur lined mittens I had in the saddlebag and put them on. I had taken my flannel blanket from my bedroll and wrapped it over my coat and brought Jeb in close and under the blanket so he was out of the wind. Jeb got so comfortable he started dozing off. Seeing Jeb so relaxed and enjoying the comforts of the blanket almost made me laugh. I knew I was close to what remained of Fort Vasquez, and when I passed it the first time on the way to Keota; I knew several buildings were still standing. If we could make the fort before nightfall, it would provide shelter until the storm passed.

Cinder's was doing all the hard work as she moved steadily and grudgingly through the snow and cold. The blizzard towards the end of the day was an almost whiteout and just when I thought we must have missed and rode on pass the old trappers fort a chipped and brown stucco wall appeared seemingly out of nowhere not more than 20 feet in front of Cinders. It was as if Cinders had read my mind and knew exactly where we were headed. Following the wall eastward then once we found the corner we followed the wall south until we came across the front gates. The old stockade gates were now long gone since they had abandoned the fort over 30 years ago. Pushing Cinders inside the walls of the fort help tremendously in keeping the northern wind at bay. I was already starting to feel better about our chances of surviving the storm.

Locating the old stable within the fort and attached to it was the horse wrangler's quarters, which was perfect for what we all needed. The stable doors were still intact and operated with a lot of pushing, grunting, and shoving. Unpacking and moving everything inside of the wranglers quarters, Jeb and I returned to see that Cinders needs were taken care of first. She had done a hell-of-a-job getting us here and out of the storm. I brushed her done with my wooden curry comb, spending some extra time working her over, making sure she was dry and warm. Luck was riding the high horse this late afternoon as there was some left over hay in the stable, and not from 30 years ago. The hay left inside was not fresh, but it was not moldy either. It would seem someone had used this very spot for shelter as recent as in the last couple of weeks and had left some of their hay behind. Fed some grain to Cinders that had been bought in Keota and after making sure she was in the best shape possible for the night, I gave her a small treat of store-bought sugar that she liked.

Once inside the horse wrangler's quarters I set my saddlebag, gunny sack full of trail grub, greener shotgun, and Winchester rifle in the corner. Having done that I took a gander of the shack and was surprised that there was an abundance of wood and dry cow chips for a fire. Since I was losing the light of the day quickly, I got a fire started in the fireplace in the old shack. It took several minutes, but soon Jeb and I both felt the heat of the fire. The heat as the room warmed was causing some odd and eerie sounds as the wood of the old building creaked and moaned as the room heated. The fire lit the room better, and I got a look see of our new headquarters to sit out the storm. There were 6 cots with cornhusk mattresses, one table, and 2 chairs. A skilled wood craftsman had made both the table and the chairs. It was a shame to see them abandon here so far from anyone that might appreciate the workmanship.

Too tired to make a decent supper Jeb and I ate a cold supper of hardtack and jerky then I laid out my bedroll on one cot. Sitting down, Jeb and I finished a full canteen of cold water. With the snow and a fire - water would not be an issue. The fire and warmth had made Jeb and me both sleepy. Laying down with my head up against the wall, Jeb jumped up on the cot and cuddle up under my blanket with his head laying on my chest. Jeb went to sleep in no time as I petted his head. As I laid there I got to thinking about what I knew about Fort Vasquez. After some pondering, some of it came back to me.

In 1835 fur-traders Louis Vasquez and Andrew Sublette built the fort along the South Platte River for the Rocky Mountain Fur Company with a license to trade with the Cheyenne and Arapahoe Indians. The fort was strategically located between Fort Laramie, to the north and Bent's Fort to the south, along the Trapper's Trail. When the price and demand for beaver pelts declined the fort was then sold and then soon after abandoned in the 1840s, over 30 years ago. Looking about at the dust and dirt, I was thankful that we could use it on this cold, blistering evening.

Listening to the blizzard as the cold northern wind howl outside, I watched the shadows created by the fire as they danced their slow death upon the walls of this old room, and my eyes grew heavy.

CHAPTER 2

Jolting awake, I tried to clear my mind. Something woke me; after a few seconds of getting the cobwebs shook loose, I realized it was Jeb that had woke me up. Jeb was laying across my chest and he was in a low growl and looking towards the one and only door of the old horse wrangler's shack. The fire had died down and the only light was the orange glow of the dying embers that were left inside the hearth of the fireplace. Now that I was fully awake I said in a low voice, "I am up now buddy."

Jeb moved cautiously off my chest as I swung my legs over the edge of the cot, reaching behind me I grabbed one of my Smith & Wesson Schofield 45's. Jeb was focused on the door, knowing it was the only entrance into the room. There were no windows, and I was solely relying on Jeb's senses. And it was obvious things were not as they should be. Since the fire was almost dying out, it was almost pitch black in here. Deciding I needed more light, I stood slowly and as silent as I could; I added some wood to the fireplace.

Having done that and with my pistol still in my hand, I sat back on the cot and watched Jeb as he watched the door. Trying to hear what he was hearing, I concentrated on listening to what lay beyond the walls of this room. All I could hear was the howl of the blizzard. There was no soft relaxing harmony to the storm outside, the wind sounded angry and I could feel the walls heave with each gust of the northern wind. Jeb stood up and he moved in a stalk towards the door. I followed him, deciding I would open the door and hoping that it was not a wolf or a mountain lion seeking shelter from the blizzard.

Pistol in my right hand, I reached with my left hand to remove the wooden plank that was locking the door when I heard a horse snort, not once, but several times. Was Cinders loose and in trouble? Now worried about my horse, I quickly threw up the wooden plank as Jeb went to barking when a gust of wind blasted the door inward. It took several seconds for the swirling snow to settle and I could finally make out what had bothered Jeb; and what I saw startled me. It was 2 horses and 2 men and they all look as if they were having a rough night in the blizzard. The first man tried to dismount and fell face first with a cushioned thud into the deepening snow. The 2nd man was able with considerable effort to dismount without falling, and I could barely hear him above the pounding wind when he said, "My brother and I smelled wood smoke and followed the smell!"

Holstering my Smith & Wesson Schofield, I pushed my way into the whiteout towards the man that had fallen and now was struggling to get up. The 2nd man and I had gotten the one that had collapsed to stand and we half carried and half dragged him into the horse wrangler's quarters.

Once inside the old shack I shut the door and slammed the locking plank into place, and then quickly threw some more wood onto the fire. With the growing fire, the room was lit better and I could finally get a good look at the strangers. The one that had collapsed looked to be about 25 years old with dark brown hair and the one that had helped me carry him in looked to be about 30 years old with similar hair color. The older brother was quickly stripping off the coat of the younger one as he moved him closer to fire. The younger brother was shivering and had goosebumps on his arms as his older brother rubbed his arms trying to get the blood flowing to his hands, which were an icy blue. The older brother spoke reassuringly to his younger brother who just opened his eyes for the first time since he had been inside, "Joe, we got a warm shack with a nice warm fire to ride out the rest of the storm. We are going to be okay, thanks to this gentleman."

The older brother looked at me and said, "The blizzard caught us by surprise with no cover. We sure as hell would be dead if not for the wood smoke. It was a miracle we could follow the smell here. Thank you much mister for giving us a hand. We will forever be in your debt. My name is Sam and my little brother here is named Joe."

If not for me finding this old fort during the blizzard, I would have been in the same boat as these 2 fellows. Pointing toward a gunny sack and then my saddlebag in the room's corner, I said, "There is beef jerky in my saddlebag and some hardtack in the gunny sack if you are hungry, you are welcome to it. While you tend to your brother, you should eat, and warm yourself, I will see that your horses are taken care of. My name is Dale, and the sad-looking mutt on the cot is named Jeb."

When I introduced Jeb I had pointed at him. Finally, noticing him for the first time since we all had made it back inside and I thought it was odd that Jeb had positioned himself on the cot. Normally if someone was injured or sick, he was right always right there in the way being a pest and trying to comfort them. Still thinking it was a tad odd of my dingo as I put my coat, hat, and wolf fur mittens on. Now bundled up against the cold, I was ready to gather up Sam and Joes horses and put them up with Cinders. One last look at Jeb before going back outside; Jeb was looking straight at me.

Both Sam and Joe's horses were jittery since they did not know me, but they let me gather their reins. The snow was too deep, and both horses were too tired to bolt. Pulling gently on their reins, I trudged through the snow leading them to the stable. Cinders seemed excited to have some new friends to sit out the storm with, and she flipped her tail and pawed the ground with her right front hoof. Taking both saddles off the horses and then I took the time to curry comb them both down. After feeding them some hay and I then fed them some of my grain. Once I was done seeing to the stranger's horse's needs I gave Cinders some extra loving so she would feel special. As soon as all the horses had been cared for - I started back to the horse wrangler's shack.

Halfway in between the stable and the old wooden shack, I stopped. Leaning into the wind trying to stand still for a minute as I surveyed the frigid whiteout of the Lord's creation before me. The wind gusts were coming in waves and in between each wave I would stumble slightly forward until the next wave, then I would have to lean back in to it to stand my ground. It made me feel alive with each frosty breath. It also made me feel trivial in the world compared to nature and the forces it could throw at you. Feeling lucky enough to find this old fort and the shelter it provided to sit out the storm, I took another deep breath of cold air and snow then moved towards the door of the shack.

Leaning on the door with my shoulder when another gust of wind attacked the door just as I pushed and with both forces working together slammed the door inward and open. With the door suddenly flying open, I stumbled and fell to my knees into the shack. Jeb barked and growl. Feeling awkward and stupid, I chuckled. Bringing my head up to see if Sam and Joe were laughing when I saw Joe still with the shakes and shivers sitting in one chair by the fire with my blanket over his shoulders and pointing my Greener shotgun straight at me. Moving my head slowly towards where Jeb was making such a racket, I saw that they had tied him to the table leg with a stout piece of rawhide. Behind him and just out of reach of Jeb's snapping jaws set Sam in a chair pointing a Colt 45 in my direction and holding the telegram that Oscar Polichio had sent me asking for my help.

CHAPTER 3

The disadvantage that I was in at this very moment, I had experienced nothing like it before in my life. I was on my knees with my own Greener shotgun pointed at my head not 20 feet away. The man holding it was sick and had the shivers, and I knew that shotgun had a light trigger. They had tied Jeb, my dingo, and my partner to the table with a stout rawhide strap and was of no use to me in any confrontation. My Smith & Wesson Schofield 45's were holstered, but under my coat, as was my bowie knife. My eyes looked pass the Colt 45 that Sam was pointing at me and locked onto his eyes when I said with a lot of malice in my tone, "What the hell is going on here?"

Sam looked upset and determined as he motioned with the barrel of his pistol, "Getting cold in here, Mr. Patton. Move forward slowly on your knees far enough into the room until you can shut the door."

Pissed was not even close to how I felt, but seeing no other choice at the moment, I did what Sam asked. Moving far enough into the room, I slowly reached behind me and shut the door, but a gust of wind blew it back open as it slammed into my back. Sam reacted by saying, "Mr. Patton I need you to do this slowly, I went you to rock back on your knees into a sitting position on the floor and then scoot back into the door so your back and body is holding the door closed."

The whole time since entering back into the horse wrangler's shack Jeb was growling and lunging at Sam. Sam was obviously distraught and as I was moving into a sitting position as I was told to do Sam shifted the barrel of his pistol and pointed it at Jeb—and then he cocked the Colt. Seeing that he was getting ready to shoot my partner I said in a loud voice, "JEB NOT NOW!"

Jeb immediately quit barking and with his hackles still raised sat down on his end gate now looking towards me waiting for another command. Sam still had his weapon pointed at Jeb and I quickly added, "No need to shoot the dog he will be quiet now! Now tell me what is going on here."

Sam hesitated and then shifted his eyes and the gun back so it was pointed at me. Now that the attention was not on Jeb, my dingo moved closer to the table which provided slack in the rawhide strap that was binding him to the table. Jeb took it in his mouth and slowly started to chew on it as if he knew he could not bring Sam's attention back on him. Jeb was trying to free himself. Sam's full attention was now back on me and he quickly raised the telegram and shook it slightly so I could see what he was holding before he spoke, "It would seem Mr. Patton that fate and destiny and this damn blizzard has dealt a poker hand that now needs to be played out."

Glancing quickly back and Joe and my Greener shotgun he had pointed at me, I could see the shotgun wavering up and down and Joe's eyes fluttering as he tried to stay awake. It would seem he would either accidently let loose the double-ought-buck or fall asleep—maybe both. Both Sam and Joe had to be exhausted from nearly freezing and after trudging through the blizzard looking for shelter. They had had no time since being here to get any sleep. They both being over tired would either get Jeb and I killed or it could be to our advantage. Looking back at Sam and still with malice in my voice, "Still not following, you are going to have to clarify it a tad better."

Sam leaned forward in his chair still holding Oscar's telegram and still pointing his Colt at me and he said in a clear and loud voice, "I got a telegram just like this only 4 days ago, but mine said that my youngest brother had been tracked down by 2 men and then shot and killed. That is what mine said, Mr. Patton. My brother Joe and I hit the trail to settle this matter. One of the men that killed my brother Tom was named in the telegram, and the other was not. The one named in the telegram was Oscar Polichio, a sod buster from Keota. While looking for the grub you offered I came across this telegram and lo-and-behold it names you Dale Lee Patton, the famous bounty hunter as the 2nd man that had taken part in the killing of our little brother. Yes, Patton, I have heard of you and I know that you are a very dangerous man. I always thought you stayed on the west slope of the Rocky Mountains, but here you are on the plains of Colorado and guilty of killing my brother. ARE YOU GOING TO DENY IT?"

It never crossed my mind that Tom Foster the killer of Annie Polichio was kin to the Foster Bandits. I had never heard of Tom until I got the telegram from Oscar. Sam and Joe Foster were a different matter altogether. They were famous in their own right and had robbed more banks in southwest Colorado than anyone. Their range included New Mexico and Arizona, but mostly they stayed down in the San Luis Valley. They were ruthless, and they left dead bodies in their wake. They had no qualms about killing those that tried to thwart their bank robberies. It would seem their younger brother had followed in their footsteps. What happens here in the next few minutes or hours I did not have the upper hand, but I knew one thing. That I would die trying to prevent these assholes from reaching Keota and cause harm to Oscar and his family. Knowing I had to wait for the right moment, I had to be careful in what I said and in a loud tone to match Sam's, "Your little brother raped and killed my best friend's 14-year-old daughter. And there is no denying I helped Oscar track down your brother and stood by as my friend shot down your brother in a fair gunfight. Or maybe that telegram you got never told you that part. Your brother happily confessed prior to his death, and when you act in how he did, there are consequences to those actions. He died standing up, I have to give him credit for that."

Jeb was gnawing at his rawhide restraint and doing so in a way that did not draw attention to himself. The dingo was by far the cleverest dog I had ever known.

Joe was having bouts of shivers and I was worried that with the light trigger of the Greener he would just shiver or nod off and blow me away by mishap instead of by design. Sam pondered on what I had said for a spell before he answered, "I get that. Tom was foolish and never the sharpest tool in the shed, but he was kin. It is just Joe and I can't have some sodbuster and bounty hunter killing our relations without repercussions. It is nothing personal Patton, it is just the way it is."

The blizzard still raged outside, and I could feel the cold as it seeped through the wooden door and my coat. I could also feel the gusts of wind as they hammered the door like ocean waves pounding a coastal shore, trying to slam it open again. The fire was dying down and just like Joe, Sam's eyes were growing heavy as the night wore on. I had to keep him talking.

Think Dale! Think! Not every situation was hopeless as they seem. My biggest advantage was that Joe and Sam were exhausted from the night in the storm and not thinking straight. It was obvious they had not realized I was wearing my pistols because of the low light given off by the fire in the shack's darkness and that my Smith & Wesson Schofield 45's were mostly hidden by my coat or they would have disarmed me by now. Jeb was still gnawing on the rawhide restraint and knowing my dingo the way I knew him. As soon as he could he was going for Sam.

Still looking at Sam, I chuckled slightly, "You know calling Oscar a sodbuster like he is a man that can't take care of himself is a huge mistake. His farm is set up like a fortress, and I doubt that you would ever sneak up on him without him ever knowing it. I would almost pay money to see you and your brother try."

Sam rolled his sleepy eyes in disbelief and replied, "Every sodbuster we have ever killed had no gumption, no sand, and zero courage. This Polichio fellow will be no different. Once confronted he will cower and beg for the life of his family and himself. We will not spare him or his family. You both killed our brother, and that makes it a blood feud. You of all people should understand that, Patton. I heard tales of how you got into the bounty hunting business, because Cash Jackson killed your wife. Enough talk I need some sleep!"

As Sam raised his pistol, aiming at me for a killing shot; Jeb had finally chewed through the rawhide and without a sound launched his full body at Sam. Spontaneously rolling to my left and away from Sam and Jeb the wind did what I hope it would do and blew the door open with a frigid gust of wind and blinding swirling snow.

Sam fired and his bullet embedded into the wooden door in mid-swing as it slammed open. Jeb's sudden attack sent Sam over backwards in his chair, banging him onto the floor with Jeb going for his face. Jeb's attack on Sam distracted Joe and shifted his attention and gaze in that direction, and by the grace of the "Lord all Mighty" he did not fire the Greener shotgun. Rolling I fumbled lifting my coat and drew my right hand Schofield and once I rolled into a position of facing the interior of the room, I fired once at Joe. He never saw it coming, as the bullet lodged itself in his upper chest. The 45 slug in such close quarters punched Joe over backwards, pounding him with a thud onto the floor. Once Joe had been shot he twitched and the Greener exploded into a deafening roar as it fired harmlessly through the now open door before he hit the floor dead.

Jeb was swarming all over Sam as I struggled to get to my feet. Looking to Joe and seeing he had not moved and was still down, I now turned my focus on the other brother. Sam still had his pistol gripped in his hand as he fought with Jeb, trying to protect his face. Once I had both pistols drawn, I said in a loud and clear voice, "JEB STOP!"

Jeb did as I asked, and he hastened to my side. The dingo's hair was still standing on end as he low growled, still looking at Sam Foster. Foster was now looking down the barrels of both of my Smith & Wesson Schofield's and thanks to Jeb, I now had the upper hand on the man that just moments ago was going to kill me in cold blood.

Foster was still flat on his back and his face was masked in blood with the damage that Jeb had caused. Foster knowing he was beat - he reluctantly let go of his Colt pistol and it fell with a thud onto the wooden floor. With my right-hand pistol still pointed at Foster, I holstered my left hand Schofield. Using my now free hand to shut the door, I then placed the wood plank in its slot to keep the door from being flung open again with the gusting wind. Foster in a panicky voice asked, "What now, Patton?"

Narrowing my eyes at this man that would have not have had a 2nd thought after he had killed Jeb and me, "Not sure Foster. I am pondering what to do with you."

The light was dim as the fire shadows on the wall were slowly disappearing into the darkness. The fire was once again dying out. Keeping one of my weapons on Sam Foster, I stepped over his dead brother Joe and I used my free hand to add more wood to the fire. The dried wood caught immediately and flared up and in a short time the wrangler's shack had light to see by. The fire shadows on the wall grew larger as I decided what needed to be done.

Sam Foster would have shot Jeb and me down in cold blood. When the weather had cleared, he would have moved on to Keota and killed Oscar and his family. Deciding there would be no arrest, no judge, no jury, and no day beyond tonight. With Jeb still glued to my side, I motioned towards Foster with my pistol, "Sam, I want you to stand slowly and I mean slowly!"

With confusing flooding the bandit's face, he did what I asked him to do, and he rolled to his side and pushed himself to his knees and then slowly stood up. Now I could get a better look at the man. Jeb in short order had done a number on his face. Foster's left earlobe was missing and droplets of blood dripped to his shoulder. His left cheek and been savagely bitten by the dingo and it was still oozing blood which trickled onto Foster's chest. Jeb when needed could be brutal to our enemy's.

Sam Foster was now standing facing me not over 25 feet away. With hatred in his tone, "Now what?"

"Slowly reach down and pick up your Colt with 2 fingers on the butt of the gun."

"What? Why?"

"I am going to give you what you would not give me. I am going to give you a chance."

"What the hell are you talking about, Patton?"

"You fired once. You still have five in the wheel. I want you to pick up your pistol and put it in your holster. Once that is done we are going to settle this once and for all."

Foster was silent as the wind continued to gust outside. His eyes told the story though, he was scared. Probably for the first time he feared for his life. Clearing his voice and just above a whisper he said, "How do I know you will not shoot me as soon as I touch the pistol?"

"You don't, but right now Foster, it is the only option you have!"

Foster hesitated, but did as I had instructed. He slowly picked up his Colt and placed it in his holster. Once he was armed and ready - I holstered my weapon to even the odds. Foster was petrified, I could see it in his eyes. He had never been in a fair fight in his life, and he was afraid. We stood like that for a spell with our eyes locked on one another—when I winked at him. Seeing my wink Fosters fear left his face and was replaced with anger. In that moment of anger, he went for his gun.

Sam Foster never cleared leather as I quick palmed both of my Schofield's and fired one from each of them. Both slugs hit home not a quarter of an inch apart in the center of Fosters chest. Foster knees buckled and in the smoke filled room his knees buckled and he collapsed slowly. First to his knees and then he flopped onto his side with a solid thump, still alive and looking at me.

Sam Foster's life was fading fast from his eyes. I bent down slowly so Foster could hear me, "You might wonder why I even gave you a chance when you would not give me one. Righteous or not; blood feud or not; you never had a chance. You can't beat a faster draw!"

Kurt James

PATTON BOUNTY HUNTER 7th Adventure

CHAPTER 1

My eyes snapped open, and it surprised me it was dark - really dark. How many hours I had laid here I had no idea, obviously a good part of a day and at least part of the night since darkness had fallen. My head was pounding and my heart was beating a drum, as I reached up and touched the left side of my face and then higher up a bullet graze just above my ear. The blood on the side of my face had dried, but the wound itself was wet to my touch as the lesion still was exuding a discharge of blood. Feeling both lucky and unlucky; unlucky in that someone had shot me, lucky that I was still alive!

Jeb had his head on my chest as I looked up at the moonless night because of the cloud cover. Seeing me awake, the cinnamon-colored short-haired Australian born dingo whimpered quietly as he showed his concern for my well-being. Knowing I needed to reassure him, I tried to reach with my left hand to pet him. In doing so, I realized I was still holding on to Cinders reins. Cinders was my blood bay three-year-old mare and when she saw me stirring she snorted and used her hoof to paw the ground. It would seem when I had tumbled out of the saddle I had the wherewithal to keep her reins clenched in my hand. Cinders moved in closer and dropped her head within inches of my face as if she was seeing for herself I was still alive, "Thanks for checking girl, I am still alive or at least I think so."

Cinders snorted twice, acknowledging my statement, and then lifted her head. Still needing to comfort Jeb, I tried to pet him, but was having difficulty moving my left arm. I had to focus on the task and hoped that the plunge had broken nothing. Moving my fingers gingerly and then my left arm and then the right one. I was sore as all get out and after moving both my legs I decided the plummet from the saddle had broken nothing, although I felt as if I just had the crap kicked out of me.

Lifting my head to sit up, a wave of dizziness flowed over me, realizing now was not the time to attempt such a maneuver I laid my head back down. Letting the spinning lights in my head to simmer down, I tried to recall what the hell happened.

My thinker had a fog, and I closed my eyes and tried to remember. I had picked up a bounty for a man named Larvin Franklin who was wanted for the killing of Probate Judge Ellis Dryer in his own courtroom in Granite, Colorado. Judge Dryer, a son of a well-known minister John Lewis Dryer, had been a respected man who had presided over some litigation for water and land rights. After his ruling in favor of one side - the losing side ramrodded by Will Franklin, the largest cattle rancher in the area ambushed and killed him. It was said Larvin, his oldest son, was the one that executed the judge. Which did not please the Colorado Territorial Governor, who was worried they would deny their bid for statehood because of the lawlessness. The Governor felt the need to place a wanted alive $500 bounty on the head of young Larvin.

Will Franklin and several other ranchers had formed a vigilante committee to right the wrong of what they saw as unjust rulings by Judge Ellis Dryer and the courts. Larvin became a "regulator" for his father in what was now being called by the newspapers in Denver as the Lake County War. The conflict ultimately turned into a test of law and justice. The Governor himself had sent me a telegram asking me to track down and capture Larvin Franklin. My intention was to bring young Larvin in alive just like the Governor wanted.

It was early winter, but the northern snows had not come yet and I took this as a good omen to track down and capture Larvin before winter took hold. I was hoping to make it back up around Montrose before the first big snow storm of the year.

Word of my arrival and my aim to bring in young Larvin had reached the Rolling Thunder Ranch at the base of West Buffalo Peak prior to my arrival. The Rolling Thunder was owned by none other than Will Franklin, the father. How word of my arrival reached the ranch before I did, I probably will never know. Some of those that rode for the Rolling Thunder brand waited in ambush for me.

To the best of my recollection, it was an hour past midday when I had wandered westward on the road that brought me to the waylay site. They always say you will never hear the crack of the rifle that fired the bullet that kills you. At first it felt as if I had been elbowed in the head—hard. Then the throbbing of the searing heat of the bullet that made the deep furrow along my scalp, all before I heard the report of the rifle.

As with all head wounds, this had bled angrily as I turned Cinders around eastward and gave her my spurs leaving my hat in the dust. In the distance I could see the snowcapped peak of Mount Oxford, knowing there would be deep dark timber at the base and such timber could provide cover to hide in. Jeb even with his short legs had kept up with Cinders as if he had known we were in a race for our lives.

Closing my eyes I could feel the cold frosty air as I sucked it into my lungs as I tried to recall more of what had happened. My head had pounded something fierce with each jarring hoof beat during Cinders bolt for the trees. During my retreat to the dark timber I tried to turn to look over my shoulder at those that pursued us, and in doing so I almost blacked out and my eyesight had faltered. In fear that I would pass out and fall from the saddle I had to turn my head back to the front and then and only then did my eyesight clear. Realizing the wound was severe I knew we had to find a place to hide for I was in no condition to fight those behind me.

Another wave of pain washed over me and for several seconds it felt as if I had been hit by lightning and from my head to toes I twitched. Gritting my teeth, I waited until the spasm had stopped before I opened my eyes again and looked upwards into the night sky. Trying to remember more of what happened became more difficult. I vaguely remembering reaching a stand of timber and not much more after that. Obviously those that had shot me had not found me, for I would now be dead. It would seem that Cinders and Jeb had known what was expected and had eluded my assassins. Having done that, they stayed and stood guard over me as darkness finally overtook the mountains.

Still lying flat on my back I looked about and even in the darkness I could see that we had ended up in a small meadow before I finally dropped out of the saddle. Come daybreak we would be easy to spot for those that wanted me dead. We needed to move out of this meadow and into a better hiding spot. Gingerly rolling from my back to my stomach and taking a deep breath, I push myself to my knees. A wave of pain and dizziness washed over me, and I closed my eyes until it passed. When the lights quit spinning behind my eyelids, I opened them and my eyesight stayed clear. Cinders had moved into a position right next to me so I could grab the stirrup of my saddle. With an all-or-nothing effort, I pulled myself up, so I was standing upright. Sort of—in an upright position. My balance was not as it should be, and I had a severe lean to the left. Taking hold of the saddle so I did not fall, I leaned my body into Cinders, taking some weight off of my legs. Been able to stand, I thought of my weapons and I could see the butt ends of my Winchester rifle and Greener shotguns were sticking up above in the slanted scabbards on each side of Cinders. My 50 caliber Sharps was still in the scabbard that rode crossways on Cinders nearside. Reaching down and then looking just to make sure both of my Smith & Wesson Schofield 45's were in their holsters. Not sure I was up to a gunfight, but at least I still had all my weapons.

Knowing there was no way in hell I could get into the saddle without tumbling face first into the meadow grass. I spoke in a quiet voice to Cinders, "Girl, I do not have the strength or agility to get in the saddle, so I need you to slowly move out towards that tree line over yonder. I am just going to hold on and use you as a crutch for now."

Cinders snorted twice and did as I asked, as she crept forward into the cold of the night. Jeb stayed close to my side as if he was standing guard. I had to focus on lifting my legs one at a time, trying to walk. Each step of picking my foot up and then setting it back down sent a jolting spasm of pain shooting all the way to the top of my noggin; each stride reminded me of the piss poor shape I was in right.

The effort of walking was taking its toll on me and after about 30 yards I started getting dizzy again. When the 2nd wave of wooziness flooded over me since standing I overstepped and then stumbled losing my grip on the saddle. And in an attempt to grab hold of the saddle to regain my balance, I fell—hard.

CHAPTER 2

I felt the cold nose of Jeb as he pressed it to my cheek, opening my eyes slowly I rolled my head to look at him and he broke into the dingo smile of his as he licked my face once. Once I saw him and his smile, I looked past him and I saw a log wall. A log wall? I was in a log cabin? Sitting up way too fast for a man that had a deep head wound, I almost passed out. Then I heard a voice like rain drops on grass, "Now don't go jerking you head around to fast and tear out all my needlework."

Reaching up, I touched my head where I had been grazed by the bullet and someone had stitched it. As the pain subsided from my throbbing head my eyes cleared as I turned toward the woman's voice. I had to blink 4 or 5 times, for I did not believe what I saw, because for sure it was an angel. An exquisite angel. She was Indian and was the spitting image of my mother Walk With Ghost when she was younger. She was petite, but walked around the cabin with the stride of one that had strength and purpose. Her dark black hair was almost to her waist as she added wood to the swaying fire in the fireplace. After she was satisfied with the amount of wood she had added, she then turned towards me and her face was flawless when she spoke, "My name is Aiyana and this is my home."

Aiyana was a beautiful name, and it summed her up well. I was so confused with at first seeing her, then baffled that I had been doctored and taken care of. It amazed me I was still alive. My throat was dry when I spoke, "How did I get here? And where exactly is here?"

Aiyana moved closer to me and then took a chair from the table and set it next to the cot I was on. Sitting down gracefully, she gently laid the back of her hand on my forehead, "Your fever has broken. You are here in my home, because your dog came to the door of my cabin 6 days ago and raised such a ruckus I thought he might have the dog sickness. He never tried to bite me, he would just bark and ran back and forth and then he got behind and he kept bumping into my legs as if he was herding me. Once I realized he was trying to get me to follow him - I did. Following your dog, I found you and your horse at the edge of the meadow just below my cabin. Once I saw you had been shot and were in such terrible shape, I returned to my cabin and got my mare Iroquois and my travois I use to haul my pelts. Once I got you rolled unto the travois, Iroquois dragged you here. Once here at the cabin I tended to your wound by cleaning and stitching it. Been spoon feeding you stew and broth for days, hoping it would keep any infection from setting in. You developed a fever on the 2nd day, today it seems it has run its course and you now are on the mend. Your horse and dog have made themselves right at home here while the spirits decided if you should live or die. I put your horse up in my shed with mine. Your guns are right here next to your bed, it was my thought you are a man that would like to have his weapons close. Other than you were wounded and in need, the only thing I know about you is that you have a beautiful, well-taken care of horse, and a dog that loves you like no other. Until now that was enough, but now I would like to know your name."

Aiyana offered me a cup of cold water which I drank greedily before answering, "My horse's name is Cinders, the dog that apparently that saved my life once again is named Jeb, and my name is Dale Lee Patton. And I am grateful for all that you have done for not just me, but Cinders and Jeb."

Jeb had jumped up on the cot and snuggled in close and found a comfortable spot and closed his eyes. Within seconds, he was snoring peacefully.

I handed back the empty cup to Aiyana and after hearing my name she set back and a look of concern crossed her face before she asked, "Dale Lee Patton the bounty hunter and gunfighter?"

"Yes, I am a bounty hunter. Cotton little to the handle of being called a gunfighter, but I have been called that by others. Do I sense regret now that you know who I am?"

Aiyana took the cup offered and then reached over and set it on the table as her eyes showed she was deep in thought, "If I had known who you were when I first when saw you laying in the meadow, I might have had second thoughts about helping. I have seen too much violence and misery in my life to want to invite that into my home. In the 6 days that you have been here, I respect the man who cares for and loves his horse and dog. No, I do not regret helping you, Mr. Patton."

Over the next 7 days, Aiyana doctored me and looked after me as I regained my strength and balance. On the 8th day since waking up in the care of this angel, I felt well enough to help with the chores of haying and grooming of not only Cinders but also Aiyana's horse Iroquois.

After locating the supplies and tools, I went to the labor of repairing Aiyana's corral that had long been neglected. My gut instinct told me I was being watched, and I turned and I saw Aiyana watching me from the doorway of her cabin as I worked, and there was a smile on her face. A smile like I used to see when my departed wife Patricia smiled at me. Our eyes locked for a spell, and it seemed that both of us were lost in thought as we looked at each other. I wondered what she was thinking at that moment. After a full minute of looking deep within each other - Aiyana returned to her daily chores.

On the 9th day since waking and the 15th day since being in Aiyana's care, I was able to shoot a large buck. While out hunting, I practiced my draw with both of my Smith & Wesson's. At first I was and felt a little shaky, but my quickness came back and after the 5th practice draw, I again felt the confidence of my ability to quick palm my pistols.

Knowing I was almost completely healed, I knew soon I would have to be on the trail. Leaving Aiyana was not something I wanted to ponder on right now. Pushing that thought to the back of my mind I went to fetch Aiyana's travois to haul the already gutted buck back to the cabin. I wanted to jerk some meat for Aiyana before the hard snows came.

After loading the buck Jeb and I started back to the cabin and I almost was overcome with emotion, an overwhelming feeling of peacefulness. A sense of belonging that I had not had since Patricia had been killed. I pulled back on Cinders reins and brought her to a halt as I ponder on why that was. These days with Aiyana had been perfect as we talked late into the night. We spoke of many things and even of our past loves and failures of love. Her husband had gone trapping over 3 years ago to never return. The Rocky Mountains had so many ways to make a man vanish into its mountain mist such as a fall from a horse, mountain lion, bear, wolf, or even the worse predator of all—man. I am sure with a woman such as Aiyana waiting at home her husband would not have just abandon her, that the Rocky Mountain frontier in one form or another had killed him. My mind was a jumble as I thought of Aiyana and at night when she went to her bed on the other side of the cabin from my cot, I struggled to find sleep no matter how tired I was. Thinking of both Aiyana and Patricia, my feelings for both were merging into one. Maybe Aiyana had not only healed my body, but maybe by being close to her for this long she had healed my heart and my soul. I know Patricia would have no hard feelings and would want me to find my happiness with another woman. Maybe now was the time. I think I was falling in love with Aiyana. Then suddenly and out of nowhere the dark thoughts of retribution flooded over the good and loving thoughts as I remembered I had unfinished business with the Franklins.

CHAPTER 3

Over the next 2 days I shot 3 more bucks and as Aiyana went to work jerking the venison as I cut firewood. I hoped to leave her with enough food and wood for the upcoming snow.

The weather the last couple of weeks was cold in the mornings, but warm sunshine in the afternoons. After doing the chores of the day and before supper Aiyana, Jeb, and I had taken walks in the forest to the meadow she found me in and after finding the perfect evergreen to sit under, we watched the ever magnificent Rocky Mountain sunset. The Lord painted for us each and every night the most beautiful orange and blue hue as the sun went to sleep on the western horizon.

Aiyana until now had never asked how I had gotten shot and ended up in her meadow dying and needing the aid of another. It was on one of our sunset walks that she finally asked. Under a darkening sky and with the moon on the rise in the east, I told her of the bounty on Larvin Franklin and how I was ambushed when I had ridden to the Rolling Thunder ranch. She then told me of her own troubles with the Franklins and the son Larvin. It would seem the younger Franklin had designs on Aiyana and as recently as a week before they shot me - he and another that rode for their brand had showed up at her cabin. Aiyana was able to fend them off after leveling her double-barrel shotgun at them. They both left, but with Larvin angrily vowing to return some day—soon. It would seem that Aiyana not only was elegant, but she had sand and was one to ride the river with. The thought of Larvin Franklin returning here and causing trouble for this woman and this place of sanctuary for me - I could not abide. Now I had more than one reason to finish what had been started on that trail not so long ago to the Rolling Thunder ranch.

On these walks I was the happiest I had been since the death of Patricia. From the way Aiyana smiled and the way she looked at me, I knew deep in my heart she felt the happiness herself. The unexpected can take you out. But the unexpected can also take you over and change your life. It would seem that the unexpected was happening to the both of us. We were finding in each other what was missing from both of our lives.

When I was working alone doing the chores of everyday living in the Rocky Mountains my mind always floated back to thoughts of Aiyana. How she walked, smiled, how the firelight at night flickered in her eyes and gave a sheen to her hair. Thinking of Patricia, there was no doubt I still loved her and that I would always love her. When Patricia had been murdered and the aftermath of my revenge trail to kill Cash Jackson, the man that had taken her life had created a hard stone in my heart. Patricia's death had changed me into a hard-edged man that could not see beyond the next bounty. Aiyana had changed how I viewed the world, I had lost my lust for life when Patricia had died. I saw that now. Aiyana had given back to me the vision I once had.

Aiyana and I had without talking about it had fallen into a routine. I would hay and see to the care of the horses as she cooked us breakfast in the mornings. Rolling out of my cot easily as to not to disturb Jeb as he slept. Standing I stretched to get the kinks of sleep out I turned to look at the dingo. Jeb was gone. What the hell? Picking up the flannel blanket and looking under it just to make sure. Then I looked under the cot and "yes" he was gone.

Baffled I walked gingerly across the one-room cabin to Aiyana's bed and in the low light of the morning I could see Jeb's nose sticking out from beneath the covers. Both Aiyana and Jeb were sound asleep. During the night the dingo had abandoned me and cuddled up with Aiyana. I stood there for several seconds taking pleasure in watching them sleep and decided I could not blame Jeb for Aiyana was one hell of a woman.

Taking the fireplace poker, I stirred last night's still glowing embers to give them the air they needed. A small flame danced as I added some wood kindling. Once I had a good warming fire going, I turned back to look at Aiyana and Jeb. What I saw put a smile on my face, for they were both awake and watching me as I tended to the fire. I felt at home here, and so did Jeb. Pointing at the dingo I said, "Are you going to slack all day and stay in bed or are you going to earn your keep around here by doing your chores?"

As Jeb and I walked out into the morning, there was a sunrise, but we did not get to bask in its glory for the clouds of an approaching storm from the north had moved in. The air had turned colder and there was frost on the evergreen needles. The trees sounded off and spoke of their misery as they snapped and crackled to the fast dropping temperature. It would seem today was the day that old man winter would make his appearance and claim the next 4 to 5 months as his own.

By the time Jeb and I had made it to the horse shed it started snowing, not little flakes; big flakes. By the time we had finished with Cinders and Iroquois there was 3 inches of heavy wet snow on the ground. The air was crisp and cold and I sucked it in deep, which made me feel alive. Looking heavenward, I stretched out my arms and l closed my eyes and opened my mouth so I could taste the snow, just like I used to when I was a kid. As long ago memories of my mother Walk With Ghost and I playing in the snow flowed through my thinker - I smiled thinking how happy I was way back then.

Still standing there enjoying the cold and the snow, I was blindsided with a snowball. Opening my eyes, I spun around and I could see Aiyana smiling, but bending over gathering up more snow for another. It would seem that she had declared a snowball war. Bending down to scoop up my own ammo, I said to Jeb, "Sic her boy!"

Jeb with his tail wagging back and forth rushed towards Aiyana in a playful and feeble attempt to "Sic her".

By the time I had finished making my first snowball, Aiyana pelted me again on the side of my noggin with her 2nd snowball. I had to hand it to her; she was a damn good shot with an excellent arm. Tossing my first snowball, it missed by a foot, flying harmlessly over Aiyana's head. Aiyana laughed out loud as she shelled me again - this time dead center of my face.

Laughing out loud myself, I knew I was being bested and would lose this snowball war; so in a last ditch effort to keep my honor intact, I did a frontal assault. In my all-or-nothing attack, I was bombarded once more before I reached Aiyana. Lowering my shoulder, I picked her up and then playfully lowered both of us down on the snow with Aiyana on her back. I was lying on top of her with our faces just inches apart and her smile evaporated as our eyes caught each other. In those exquisite brown eyes, I saw everything I would ever need again. Feeling the mist of each other's breath in the cold, Aiyana placed her right hand behind my head and slowly pulled me to her as she said in a whisper, "Kiss me."

The best feeling in the world is when you kiss someone for the first time when you really wanted to kiss them for a long time. Our kiss was deep with longing and when we parted our eyes stayed the course and we saw in each other the love that had been smoldering for some time. There was no doubt I loved this woman, and she loved me. Destiny had dropped me at her doorstep for both of us to love again. Aiyana healed me physically and spiritually, and I knew that her healing had run its course as well.

Standing slowly and holding both of Aiyana's hands, I pulled her so she was standing next to me. We forgot the heavy and wet snow that was falling all around as we both knew it was time to explore our love even more. With Jeb leading the way, Aiyana and I walked hand in hand back to the cabin.

Once inside the warm cabin breakfast was forgotten as we shed our clothes quickly. My cot was also forgotten as we crawled under the flannel blankets on Aiyana's bed. Pulling her from behind, I arched her backwards as I lifted her hair to softly kiss her neck; within minutes I could feel Aiyana's legs shudder in pure bliss and pleasure. Being in love and making love, we spent the morning hours exploring each other as if we were the only people in the world.

Aiyana and I got up at midday to make us something to eat. The morning had been wonderful and on this snow filled day some of our chores were put aside as we got to know each other. One chore that could not be put off until tomorrow was I needed to go feed and water the horses. Aiyana went about the chore of getting us fed while I got dressed.

While getting dressed Jeb stood by myside with his head turned sideways as if he was waiting for an answer to an unspoken question. Jeb in so many ways had helped me deal with the aftermath of Patricia's death. He was always there to ease my grieving when some nights it was overwhelming, he never judged me, didn't care if I was in a foul mood, and loved me unconditionally, and he had saved my life more than once. Aiyana and I being together was a huge change in the dingo's life. I know he approved, but I sense he wondered if it was forever. Patting the side of the bed indicating to Jeb that he should join me. Jeb quickly jumped up and laid his head in my lap and looked at me with his "wanting to know" eyes.

Aiyana walked over to the bed and she set down placing Jeb in between us. She reached out and gave the dingo some love as she slowly massaged him behind his ears. Aiyana then spoke, "Jeb wants to know what his future holds. He wondering if he is living here for good."

My eyes searched out and found Aiyana's eyes and I saw in them the very same question. I was so in love with this woman. Smiling I said, "You think I should break the news to him?"

"You must, now is the time to decide what the future may hold for not only Jeb, but for all of us."

Looking at Aiyana so there was no misunderstanding, "My mother told me once many years ago that if you feel it - say it. Aiyana when my wife died, I was lost – I see that now. I have been healing on the inside slowly over the last several years. Since I have been here with you I have set aside all that grief and misery that rode the trail with me. I feel that you and I belong to one another and that fate brought us together for a reason. Without knowing the other we both needed each other and destiny finally set that in motion. If I had to choose to breathe or to love you, I would use my last breath to tell you that. If you will have us - Jeb and I would like to stay."

Jeb understood full well what I had just said and he snapped his head around to wait for Aiyana's answer.

Aiyana eyes widen as they watered and a single tear slowly rolled down her face, "Dale Patton, we will be one, all of us together. Yes, Jeb and you can stay for it is within my heart that my love for you, for him, is on fire."

Jeb on hearing what he wanted to hear jumped off the bed and started doing spins on the cabin floor with his tail wagging so fast that it made us dizzy watching him. As Aiyana and I laughed at our dingo we all knew it was now official we had just become a family.

After finishing our afternoon chores, Aiyana fixed a wonderful supper that we ate by firelight. The snow had quit and our mountain retreat was silent in the aftermath of the passing storm. The cot I had spent the weeks in healing was now put away as we would now share a bed as lovers do. It felt good to have harmony in tune with my spirit once again.

CHAPTER 4

Waking up the fire was almost out, and the cabin had become cold. Jumping out of bed I quickly dressed and went to work tending the fire and stirring the ashes until I got the red-hot embers at the bottom to the top. The embers fed on the air and a small flame raised out of the soot, which I promptly added kindling to. Once the kindling took hold I added more wood, and in no time the cabin warmed up.

When Aiyana rolled out of bed I kissed her as if there was no tomorrow. When she was dressing, I strapped on my pistols, grabbed my Winchester. Living in the Rocky Mountain frontier you learn to always be armed, for there was danger in the places you never knew danger could be. Once I was well heeled I opened the door to the new morning. The sun was doing what it does best and was starting already to warm the mountains as it slowed, arced above the horizon in the east. The snow had left about 8 inches of wet snow and the Rocky Mountains from this day forward would be wet, snow packed, or muddy until spring. It was just the way it was.

After hauling fresh water from the well to the horses, Jeb and I forked them some hay and gave them some grain. After Cinders and Iroquois were watered and fed, I gave them both a good going over with the wooden curry comb. I started with Iroquois as Jeb and Cinders started touching their noses together as if they were renewing their friendship.

I spent about an hour grooming Iroquois and you could tell by the way she lifted and moved her head she was feeling fancy. Made me smile as I looked at her feeling so prideful, it reminded me of a quote by Abraham Lincoln, "I can make a General in five minutes but a good horse is hard to replace." Like him or hate him, old Abe was a man that knew his words.

Just as I put Iroquois back in her stall and before I could fetch Cinders from hers, Jeb started acting sort of peculiar as he headed to the horse shed door in a rush and paced back and forth. I had learned to trust the dingo's instincts, and I quick palmed both of my Smith & Wesson Schofield 45's one at a time and made sure I had 6 in the wheel of each. Holstering my weapons, I followed Jeb to the doorway.

Jeb's hackles raised, but he remind silent as 3 men rode passed the horse shed towards the cabin without turning to see Jeb or me. All 3 were dressed as cowhands, all were heavily armed. Although I had never seen him face to face, the one in front was none other than Larvin Franklin. The wanted poster I had in my pocket of my Levi's was a great rendering of the man wanted for the murder of Judge Ellis Dryer.

Aiyana stepped out of the cabin, holding her shotgun just as Jeb and I stepped out of the horse shed. I was behind the cowboys and Aiyana was in front of them. They still had not seen me as they focused all on Aiyana. Larvin gave a wolf whistle and then chuckled before he spoke, "You are looking mighty fine this morning, even for a squaw."

Even before Aiyana could reply, I said, "You got something to say mister, you say it to me!"

Jeb drifted to my right in an arc and closer to the Rolling Thunder ranch hands horses. The dingo was getting himself ready to disrupt their day. He would wait until I was ready.

All 3 Rolling Thunder hands fell silent. The 2 closest to me slowly turned their horses to face me. Larvin then followed suit and turned his horse again slowly to face me. Larvin raised his eyebrows as he was in deep in thought and then he asked, "Who exactly are you, mister?"

"When you ambush someone, you really should remember their face. The 2nd mistake you made is that you should find out if you actually killed them or not!"

Larvin nodded his head—yes - in acceptance, "The bounty hunter?"

"Yes, Franklin, the bounty hunter. The same one the Territorial Governor dispatched to bring you in for justice in the killing of Judge Dryer."

Franklin chuckled, "Well boys, it seems we are in the presence of a famous man. This is Dale Lee Patton, the bounty hunter. As for looking for you, Patton, thought, I tagged you pretty good in the head, we didn't search. We thought you crawled off some place to die."

"It would seem I am tougher than you thought. And just to be clear, I do not cotton to you riding up here to do whatever you had in your mind to Aiyana."

Larvin looked over his shoulder for a second at Aiyana, then back at me before speaking, "It looks like an angel saved you. An Indian angel. So, tell me, Patton are you still looking to make that $500 bounty by taking me in?"

"Aiyana is an angel, and she did save my life. Have to admit you tagged me good. It was touch and go there for a spell. As I was on the mend, I thought about that bounty on you—a lot. To answer your question, I have decided not to pursue bringing you in."

A look of confusion flooded over the face of Larvin Franklin as he pondered on what I had just said. He twitched his mouth a tad when he spoke, "Let's see if I got this right. You have decided to not to pursue the bounty? You are going to let me ride out of here without a fuss?"

"There I go - not explaining myself fully. My momma used to chastise me for that very thing. I decided not to pursue the bounty on you, I never said I was going to let you ride out of here without a fuss!"

Total silence for almost a full minute. I knew it would be Larvin that would make the first move before the other 2 Rolling Thunder hands. Just when I saw in the younger Franklin's eye that the moment of reckoning was now at hand, I yelled, "NOW JEB!"

Most of the time while in battle and you are on your feet and your opponents are on horseback, you are at a disadvantage. Having a dingo as your partner and one that is as smart as Jeb; he alone can flip your disadvantage into an asset. Jeb went after the horses - hard.

Franklin went for his sidearm just as Jeb got all 3 of the Rolling Thunder horses in a jitter trying to sidestep the dingo devil from Australia. With the same quickness I had before Franklin had shot me, I palmed both of my Smith & Wesson's. Firing from the hip. Franklin caught the first one just above his belt buckle, and the 2nd one slammed home into his upper-chest just below his neck, both shots fired so close together punched Larvin out of the saddle. My left-handed pistol I used on the man in the middle and just after he cleared leather he was slammed out of the saddle with 2 well-placed 45 slugs into his upper chest. The Rolling Thunder rider on the right was stamped out of his saddle when Aiyana let loose with both barrels of her shotgun as he attempted to draw a bead on Jeb.

Larvin and the other 2 that rode for the Rolling Thunder brand were all down in the snow and mud. All 3 men were dead. The smell of gunfire still lingered in the air as the echo of the battle slowly faded away into the distance.

CHAPTER 5

Aiyana slowly walked across what had been the battlefield in
front of her cabin to me. Folding into my arms, I felt her body
shiver, and not from the cold. Pushing her back gently so I could
see her face and look into her eyes and I could see she was in
shock of what had just happened. Threatening to shoot someone
and shooting and killing them was the line some could not cross.
Sometimes you had to cross that line and take everything a person
would ever be away from them. If you did not - then you became
prey for those looking to take an advantage. Larvin and the other 2
rode here with no good intentions; they just did not know I was
here. I hate to think what would have happened to Aiyana if she
had been here alone. One thing for sure was the woman that I had
fallen in love with had courage, sand, and strength. Pulling her
back in my arms, I tilted her head so I could kiss her. After a
lingering kiss I once again gently pushed back at arm's length and
said, "You did the right thing Aiyana, you protected your home,
yourself, Jeb, and me. These men were up to no good today, and
they were the ones that had set in ambush waiting to kill me.
Larvin Franklin is the one that shot me, by his own admission. I
know you do not want to hear this, but there is one last thing I need
to do. I am going to load all 3 of these malcontents on their horses

and take their bodies back to the Rolling Thunder Ranch. There may be those at the ranch that knew they were headed here, and they will come looking when they do not show back up. I am going to brace this head on and take the bodies back and have a say so with the man that is calling the shots at the Rolling Thunder - Will Franklin."

Aiyana folded once again back into my arms, "He will kill you!"

"It is highly possible, or he may try, or Will Franklin may be reasonable if I confront him with honor. I am hoping for the later. Whatever comes of it—I have to end this at the Rolling Thunder and not here were you would be in danger."

The sun had reached a point in the sky that day was warm enough to melt the snow. Loading the bodies proved more difficult than I had hoped for because of the slippery mud and snow. Having accomplished the task of strapping the body's crossways across their saddles, I ate a hearty meal that Aiyana prepared. I could feel the sadness of Aiyana as she moved about in silence as she cooked Jeb and I what could be our last meal. I would need the food in my belly for the strength it would provide in the daunting task of what I was planning on doing.

After getting our grub on, Jeb and I headed down from the cabin from the base of Mount Oxford in an easterly direction towards West Buffalo Peak and the Rolling Thunder Ranch. I had to give Aiyana credit, for she was strong with no tears as we kissed before I left her for a rendezvous with an uncertain outcome. We both knew in the aftermath of what was to be - that I might not be coming back.

I reckoned the distance from the cabin to the Rolling Thunder Ranch as a crow would fly was roughly 6 miles. Most of the trail would be through heavy dark timber and slow going.

Having never seen or met Will Franklin, but from my life experience here in the Rockies, I knew his type. He would be a man that had forged a cattle empire out of nothing. He would be brass, ruthless, smart, deadly, and would impose his will on others when it suited him to do so. He would be a man that would like no one telling him what to do. That was clear in the killing of Judge Dryer. He had to be all of this and more for him to accomplish what he has done here in on the Rocky Mountain frontier. He had carved his home and empire out of the wilderness, which was not for the faint–hearted. Most men like Will Franklin had a sense of honor. I hoped that by confronting him face to face that he would respect me for doing the honorable thing in bringing his son home. That it was me that had been the one that had caused the death of his ranch hands and son would not be met favorably. In case I did not make it off of Rolling Thunder land alive, I would not tell of Aiyana's role in killing one of those that rode for the brand in an attempt to protect her.

Pulling back On Cinders reins I again checked all of my weapons, Greener shotgun loaded with 2 double-ought shells, Winchester rifle fully loaded with one levered into the chamber, and my Smith & Wesson's had a full complement of 6 rounds in each. Looking skyward and not one cloud as far as I could see. There was no breeze, and the sun was shining and felt warm on my face. If this was the day that had been fated for me to die, well, hell, I could not have picked a better day for it.

At midday I rode pass where I had been ambushed without getting shot again, so far, so good. It was another mile before I could see the ranch and the entrance. On this well-traveled trail, the entrance was a stout-looking affair that framed the trail. They had constructed it of 2 huge lodge pole pine trees that were a good foot and a half around. These immense trees had been shaved of their bark and they had planted the pillars standing plumb straight up towards the heavens, and they topped out at about 14 feet tall. Laying on top of these shaved trees was another shaved tree roughly the same size that had been fitted with a lap joint on each end to connect all 3 trees. All of this sturdy workmanship had been done to support a single wooden sign that had been carved and painted to say Rolling Thunder Ranch.

Passing under the ranch sign, Cinders threw her head twice and snorted as she was leading the other 3 horses that had the bodies strapped across them on. Jeb was staying about 15 feet in front and his hackles were raised. Both Cinders and Jeb were smart enough to know we were now in hostile territory. There were several ranch hands milling about doing their daily chores, but known of them had noticed us yet. That was about to change.

When I was about 100 yards from the house a couple of ranch hands finally turned in my direction and one of them yelled out, "Toby run and get the boss, we got visitors."

A young boy near the corral turned and then sprinted toward the big house. After the first man had yelled all the ranch hands, even those on horseback that I could see turned towards me and all of them to a man started walking or riding in my direction. Doing a quick count in my head, there were 15 that I could see, possibly more that I could not see. All of them were armed. If this turned into a shooting match, there was no way in hell that I was going to survive it.

The Rolling Thunder main house was an impressive 2-story affair. There was an upper and lower porch sticking out of the front under an overhang. Stout lodge pole pillars supported both porches and the over-hang, much like the ones at the entrance of the ranch. The house had more glass windows than I have ever seen before in just one building. They had framed the rest of the house with milled lumber instead of being built with logs. This house was immense, ornamental, and expensive, and a monument to the man that owned it, a rich and powerful man.

Just as I was within 50 feet of the front porch 2 men walked cautiously out the door and stopped when they were standing on the top step. Pulling back on Cinders reins, we came to a halt. Jeb was at my side with his hackles still raised.

One man was older by a good 20 years. He was a big man, probably 6'4" and weighing in at 300 pounds. No hat, bald head, and a white unkempt mustache that had not seen a clipper in a long time. This man looked powerful and had an air of authority about him. This had to be Will Franklin. The 2nd younger man was the spitting image of Larvin and if I had to guess I would say he was another son of Will Franklin. Both wore Colt pistols tied down to their right legs.

Bad news is delivered with speed and one of the ranch hands trotted up to last horse in line and lifted the head and yelled out, "This one is Thomas, boss!" Then he hurried to the next horse and lifted the head, "This one is Boyd!" Moving even quicker, he lifted the 3rd head and in a more subdued voice, "This one is Larvin, boss!"

Will Franklin's eyes narrowed to slits as he glared at me, "Son, you better have one hell of an explanation why you are carting around the dead bodies of 2 of my best hands and my son!"

In a loud and confident voice, "This morning bright and early all 3 of these gents rode up to the Indians woman's cabin at the base of Mount Oxford. They intended to do her harm. This I could not abide and I put a stop to it."

Will Franklin was a man trying hard to control his anger, "You are telling me mister you shot and killed all of them, including my son? Why were you at the Indian woman's cabin? And who exactly are you?"

"My name is Dale Patton. I was at the Indians woman's cabin because she saved my life after you son bounced a 45 slug off my noggin not more than a mile for this very spot. Like I said earlier, your son, and the others rode to the Indian woman's cabin with no good intentions. I showed myself and when they found out who I was, then your son and the others went for their guns. And yes, I killed all three."

Will Franklin, "Dale Lee Patton? The bounty hunter?"

Nodding my head up and down, "Yes, the bounty hunter."

There was an almost silent gasp among the ranch hands that surrounded me. My reputation proceeded me and they all knew that if it came to a shooting match, some of them would die.

Will Franklin, "Larvin swore to me he had killed you!"

"Like I said, Mr. Franklin, he tried once from ambush. He tried once again this morning at the Indians woman's cabin. He will not get a third chance!"

The younger man stepped forward as anger flooded his face, "We are going to kill you Patton, gunfighter or not, you will not get out of here alive!"

As soon as the brother of Larvin said his piece, his father backhanded him so hard that the boy's shoulders hit the porch before his back. The old man stood over his son and spoke in a harsh tone, "Teddy, I will be the one who decides if there is any killing to be done and who to kill—not you!"

Teddy touched his busted lip gingerly and said, "But, Pa, you're not going to let this bounty hunter ride out of here after killing Larvin, are you?"

Will Franklin turned to face me as he answered his son, "I am pondering on what I am going to do and you or nobody else is going to push me into making a hasty call!"

You could feel the tension in the air as all the Rolling Thunder ranch hands waited for the boss to give the word and they would gun me down. If I was to die here today, so was Will Franklin and his boy Teddy. And the boss and ramrod of the Rolling Thunder knew that. He was a man of vision and he could see it in my eyes.

Will Franklin spoke loud and clear so everyone could hear him and there was no misunderstanding, "Patton, I don't much like you, nor do I like your kind. Bounty hunting for blood and money is the lowest a man can get in my eyes. Guess I didn't much cotton to Larvin either. After the boy's mother died I did my best, which was far from being good enough. Both of my pups sort of went off the reservation, so to speak. Larvin was the worse. He was rotten to the core that boy was, rotten to the core. He took it upon himself to kill Judge Dryer once he had done that - it all steamrolled downhill. He had gotten word that you - the Territorial Governor had dispatched the most famous bounty hunter in the Rocky Mountains himself to bring him in. Once again he went against my wishes and set up to kill you. He failed not once, but twice, and paid the ultimate sacrifice with his life. A man has to defend his life and honor, and you did that. I cannot fault you for that, for I would have done the same thing. As for the Indian woman, it almost shames me how Larvin lusted after that woman. Her husband had been a decent enough fellow before he disappeared. The squaw stayed and never bothered no one - she is a kind woman."

Will Franklin paused for a spell as his words sank into everyone's minds before he spoke again, "Patton, I appreciate you having the guts to bring my son home for a proper burial. For that you get a onetime pass. Larvin had it coming, I know that, but hear me boy, and you burn this into your memory. Good man or wicked man, Larvin was my son and my blood ran thick in his veins! And If I ever catch you or that mangy mutt of Rolling Thunder range again, we will shoot you on sight! Do I make myself clear?"

My eyes narrowed, and I spoke just as loud, "Crystal clear and understood Franklin. You and the rest of the Rolling Thunder hands must know that the Indian woman, her land, and her cabin are now under my protection. If any of your men get to—lusting—after her, you and they will have to deal with me. Do I make myself clear?"

Will Franklin, "Understood Patton, now get your ass off my range!"

Pulling hard enough back on Cinders reins, I backed her up while still facing Will Franklin, "Time to take our leave Jeb."

Jeb glared and barked once at Will Franklin, showing his displeasure for being called mangy. After having his say, the dingo backed up with Cinders and I. Once we cleared the circle of men surrounding us - I turned Cinders and trotted her away from Will and Teddy Franklin and the Rolling Thunder ranch.

After putting 3 miles distance away from the ranch, I halted Cinders and turned back towards the way I had just come and waited for 15 minutes. Deciding we were not being followed, I dismounted and squatted on the ground Indian style. This signaled Jeb to jump into my lap. Giving the dingo my love by roughing him up behind the ears like he enjoyed, and he deserved for all that he did for me today in both confrontations at the cabin and at the ranch. Smiling, I said, "Time to head home buddy."

Jeb grinned that dingo smile of his, because he knew "home" now was not just a direction. It meant we were heading back to the cabin and Aiyana.

Patton – Bounty Hunter - Extra

As an author of western/mystery fiction I like weave my fictional heroes into a timeline of actual events and places. All of my novels and short stories take place for the most part in Colorado. As a native son of the state I spent my formative years exploring the Rocky Mountains and learning of its history. Even to this day in all of my spare time you will find me exploring ghost towns, mining camps, and in the long lost forgotten cemeteries across the mountains. One of John Muir most famous quotes is, "The mountains are calling, so I must go" – this quote speaks to me like no other.

In my novels most of my stories occur over a wider range of Colorado. I think of these as my - trail books – as in getting from one place to another with perils along the trail. My short stories usually happen in one local area of Colorado. I wanted to expand the readers experience here with the Patton – Bounty Hunter series and give you the reader a little background on the locations of each of Dale Lee Patton, Jeb, and Cinders adventures. Just know that each town, mountain, mountain pass, mining camp, and rivers did in fact exist or in most cases still exist. I try to use the historical names, but in some instances I use the more modern name just for clarity. Here are a few fun facts of the short stories you just read.

I have included a map for you to get the basic idea of where in the Colorado the Patton – Bounty Hunter stores took place.

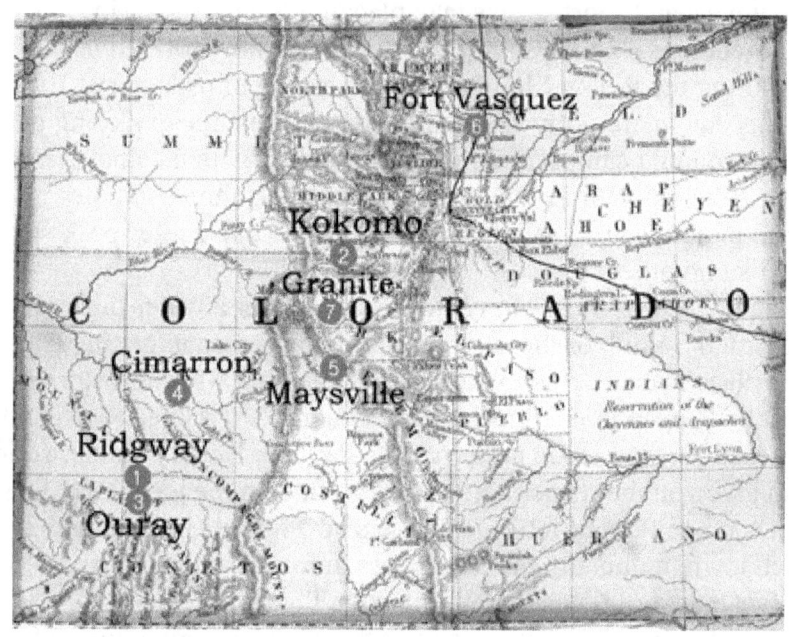

Patton – Bounty Hunter – The Beginning

#1 Ridgway, Colorado

Coordinates: 38°9′7″N 107°45′25″W- Ridgway had been coined as the Gateway to the San Juans, is in the southwestern portion of Colorado. The town is a former railroad stop on the Uncompaghre River in the northern San Juan Mountains. Steep forested mountains and cliffs surround Ridgway on the south, east, and northeast. The Uncompahgre River runs through the town. Dallas Creek also flows from the south-west and forms a confluence with

the Uncompahgre. There is a notable wildlife presence —
mountain lions, badgers, deer, elk, bears, coyotes, wild turkey, and
bald eagles are indigenous to the area. The regions bald eagles nest
in the cottonwoods along the river and are a common sight in the
late fall. Ridgway began as a railroad town, serving the nearby
mining towns of Telluride and Ouray. The town site is at the
northern terminus of the Rio Grande Southern Railroad where it
meets with Denver and Rio Grande Western Railroad running
between Montrose and Ouray.

Patton – Bounty Hunter – 2nd Adventure

#2 Kokomo, Colorado

Coordinates: 39°25′27″N 106°11′23″W - Just off I-70. Few mining
towns had an elevation greater than that of Kokomo's 10,618 feet.
Access to the town in 1878 was only by narrow trails carved out of
the side of mountains. The summer of 1879 saw Kokomo with a
population of 1500. By the year 1881, the town had grown to
10,000. It was in that year a disastrous fire nearly destroyed all of
the wooden structures in the town. Rebuilding started immediately

and it looked as if the town would regain its former place in the sun. But it did not. Some of the mines declined in production, others closed and the town gradually began to decline. Racen and Kokomo were next door neighbors, so much so that often is was difficult to know which was which. When most of Kokomo was destroyed by fire in the winter of 1881-82, what remained of Kokomo was merged with Racen. Some placer ore was found here in 1860, but little mining was done until the Leadville boom when several rich strikes were made. It is said the Dead Man claim was located when a miner dug a grave to bury a friend. The town began fading in the 1880s but has never completely died. Kokomo was named after the city in Indiana, birthplace of some of the early settlers. Racen was named for the Recen brothers, prominent in the early history of the area.

Patton – Bounty Hunter – 3rd Adventure

#3 Ouray, Colorado

Coordinates: 38°1′24″N 107°40′20″W - Originally established by miners chasing silver and gold in the surrounding mountains, the town at one time boasted more horses and mules than people. Prospectors arrived in the area in 1875. In 1877, William Weston and George Barber found the Gertrude and Una gold veins in Imogene Basin, six miles south southwest of Ouray. Thomas Walsh acquired the two veins and all the open ground nearby. In 1897, Walsh opened the Camp Bird Mine, adding a twenty-stamp mill in 1898, and a forty-stamp mill in 1899. The mine produced almost 200,000 ounces of gold by 1902, when Walsh sold out to Camp Bird, Ltd. By 1916, Camp Bird, Ltd., had produced over one million ounces of gold. At the height of the mining, Ouray had more than 30 active mines. The town—after changing its name and that of the county it was in several times—was incorporated on October 2, 1876, named after Chief Ouray of the Utes, a Native American tribe. By 1877 Ouray had grown to over 1,000 in population and was named county seat of the newly formed Ouray County on March 8, 1877. The Denver & Rio Grande Railway arrived in Ouray on December 21, 1887. It would stay until the automobile and trucks caused a decline in traffic. The last regularly scheduled passenger train was September 14, 1930. The line between Ouray and Ridgway was abandoned on March 21, 1953. The entirety of Main Street is registered as a National Historic District with most of the buildings dating back to the late nineteenth century. The Beaumont Hotel and the Ouray City Hall and Walsh Library are listed on the National Register of Historic Places individually, while the Ouray County Courthouse, St. Elmo Hotel, St. Joseph's Miners' Hospital (currently housing the Ouray County Historical Society and Museum), Western Hotel, and Wright's Opera House are included in the historic district.

Red Mountains - is a set of three peaks in the San Juan Mountains of western Colorado in the United States, about 5 miles south of Ouray. The mountains get their name from the reddish iron ore rocks that cover the surface. Several other peaks in the San Juan Mountains likewise have prominent reddish coloration from iron ore and are also called "Red Mountain". The area had several mining camps one of which was Copper Glen mentioned in the story.

Patton – Bounty Hunter – 4th Adventure

#4 Cimarron, Colorado

Coordinates: 38°26′30″N 107°33′22″W - Our knowledge of the human history of the Cimarron area prior to the 1850s is sketchy. The Tabaquache Utes may have moved through the area on their journeys between the Gunnison area east of Cimarron where they spent summers, and their winter destination, the Uncompahgre Valley to the west. In 1853, explorer John W. Gunnison's party passed through the area, searching for a possible transcontinental railroad route. The explorers were discouraged by their demanding traverse of the Lake Fork of the Gunnison River canyon to the east. They then veered over Blue Mesa and eventually made their way west, crossing Cimarron Creek and climbing over Cerro Summit. Captain Gunnison proclaimed that this rugged country was totally unsuitable for a railroad and his sentiments were echoed by other explorers who followed. As valuable mineral deposits were discovered on Colorado's western slope, the need for better transportation routes was recognized. One of the most famous road builders of his day was Otto Mears, known as the "Pathfinder of the San Juan's". Mears constructed the Lake Fork and Ouray Toll Road. A branch of this road ran from the confluence of Cimarron Creek and the Little Cimarron River to a local cattle outfit, Cline's Ranch. Captain W. M. Cline owned about 480 acres in the vicinity of what was to become Cimarron. A friend of Chief Ouray of the Utes, Cline settled here in the 1870s, raising grain and cattle. Cline was joined in the livestock business by two other firms whose herd totaled approximately 5400 head of cattle, and this area eventually became popular for sheep-raising as well. By the early 1880s, General William Jackson Palmer's railroad, the Denver and Rio Grande, was on its way west across Colorado. Palmer eagerly accepted the challenge of constructing a railroad through the Black Canyon of the Gunnison, a feat that was previously considered impossible. In August of 1882, the first D&RG train rolled out of the canyon and into the construction camp at the end of the tracks near Cline's Ranch on Cimarron Creek. During the survey for the railroad, the workers had discussed what the camp at the end of the line ought to be called. Some were reminded of the hills around Cimarron, New Mexico, and the camp was dubbed "Cimarron". When the first train arrived, the passengers were greeted by a host of tents and a single log cabin. Many believed that as the railroad continued on west, Cimarron would disappear. But by the end of 1882, it was recognized that getting trains over the steep Cerro Summit grade would require helper engines. Cimarron developed into a real railroad town, complete with a roundhouse and station facilities. The original purpose of this railroad was to provide a link for shipment of ore from the mines in the San Juan Mountains. However, scenic excursions also ran through Cimarron in the latter part of the 19th and into the 20th centuries. A subsidiary of the D&RG, the "Rio Grande Hotel Company", established the "Black Canyon Hotel and Eating House" in Cimarron. Railroad passengers came to eagerly anticipate the stop in this community known for its hospitality. Its population fluctuated drastically during this time, at times soaring to 250 or dwindling to 25.

Black Canyon, Colorado

Coordinates 38°34'0"N 107°43'0"W - The Ute Indians had known the canyon to exist for a long time before the first Europeans saw it. They referred to the river as "much rocks, big water," and are known to have avoided the canyon out of superstition. By the time the United States declared independence in 1776, two Spanish expeditions had passed by the canyons. In the 1800s, the numerous fur trappers searching for beaver pelts would have known of the canyon's existence but they left no written record. The first official account of the Black Canyon was provided by Captain John Williams Gunnison in 1853, who was leading an expedition to survey a route from Saint Louis and San Francisco. He described the country to be "the roughest, most hilly and most cut up," he had ever seen, and skirted the canyon south towards present-day Montrose. Following his death at the hands of Ute Indians later that year, the river that Captain Gunnison had called the Grand was renamed in his honor. The Gunnison River drops an average of 34 feet per mile through the entire canyon, making it the 5th steepest mountain descent in North America. By comparison, the Colorado River drops an average of 7.5 feet per mile through the Grand Canyon. The greatest descent of the Gunnison River occurs within the park at Chasm View dropping 240 feet per mile. The Black Canyon is so named because its steepness makes it difficult for sunlight to penetrate into its depths. As a result, the canyon is often shrouded in shadow, causing the rocky walls to appear black. At its narrowest point the canyon is only 40 ft. wide at the river.

Patton – Bounty Hunter - 5th Adventure

#5 Maysville, Colorado

Coordinates: 38°32'19"N 106°11'25"W - Originally known as Crazy Camp, Maysville was the conglomeration of two small camps located right next to each other. One named Crazy Camp and the other Maysville. When they merged, the town took on the name Crazy Camp but later changed it to Maysville. The town boasted the Maysville Chronicle with a circulation of over 1000 - the largest in the county. Maysville sat at the Eastern Junction of the Monarch toll pass from which two toll roads ran, one to Hancock and the other to Shavano. There were dance halls, large supply stores, a half dozen saloons, and much more in this town. A small fire took five buildings downtown in July of 1880 and the town pretty much died with the 1893 mineral price panic. Today there are many cabins in the area along with the original schoolhouse.

Poncha Pass, Colorado

Coordinates 38°25'20"N 106°05'13"W - is a mountain pass in South-Central Colorado. It lies between the San Luis Valley to the south and the valley of the Arkansas River to the north, and is one of the lowest mountain passes in the state. It is in the saddle between the Sangre de Cristo Range, lying to the southeast, and the Sawatch Range, lying to the west and northwest. Poncha Pass lies on the border between Chaffee County and Saguache County, and on the border between the San Isabel National Forest and the Rio Grande National Forest.

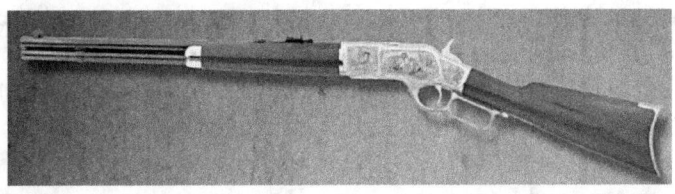

Patton – Bounty Hunter – 6th Adventure

#6 Fort Vasquez, Colorado

Coordinates 40°11'40"N 104°49'13"W - It is listed in the National Register of Historic Places and is administered by the Colorado Historical Society. In 1835 fur-traders Louis Vasquez and Andrew Sublett built the fort along the South Platte River for the Rocky Mountain Fur Company with a license to trade with the Cheyenne and Arapahoe Indians. The fort was strategically located between Fort Laramie, to the north and Bent's Fort to the south, along the Trapper's Trail. When the price and demand for beaver pelts declined the business dissolved in 1842 and was sold to the firm Locke and Randolph, who abandoned it in 1842. Foundations and a few feet of the exterior walls we all that remained by 1932. In 1934 the owners of the Fort Vasquez Ranch, Pearl Perdiew and Ethel Hoffman deeded an acre of land surrounding the fort to the Weld County Commissioners. In 1935-36, WPA crews rebuilt the walls from existing bricks on the location. Features include the rebuilt fort with guard towers, firing ledges and portals based on the best information available. In the years 1968-70, CSU students excavated more than 4,000 artifacts. Their work established the original dimensions of the fort - 100' X 98.5' and located the true foundations for the interior walls and fireplaces.

Keota, Colorado

Coordinates: 40°42'10"N 104°04'31"W - Novelist James Michener used Keota as his center of operations while writing his novel "Centennial". The area around here was also the base for the TV series by the same name. An 11 miles side trip to the Pawnee Buttes is worth the trip - Michener referred to these buttes as Rattlesnake Buttes in his book. Keota lies in the center of the Pawnee National Grasslands which covers thousands of acres of public land. Keota is not the traditional 'ghost town' one thinks of in Colorado because it is not in the mountains. However, it played a big part in the settling of the state and was a center for the vast cattle industry and later agriculture. Best times to visit are spring and fall - summer and winter can be very hot and cold respectively. You get a great feel for what it was like to be a pioneer on the Great American Desert. The prairie blooms in the spring and is truly beautiful. There aren't any facilities within 15-20 and make sure your gas tanks are full when you leave Briggsdale. A trip to the cemetery is worth the trip - 1.6 miles out of town on the main street heading east. Elevation is 4961' above sea level. 'Keota' is an Indian word meaning "Gone to visit" or "The fire goes out". It was a station stop on the 'Old Prairie Dog Express' on the Colorado-Wyoming Division of the Burlington-Missouri Railroad. Keota was established as a homestead in 1880 by two sisters, Mary and Eva Beardsley and sold to the Lincoln Land and Cattle Co. in 1888. The railroad (used mainly for cattle shipping) was abandoned and the tracks were removed in 1975. The Dean Bivens family, who maintained the roads, are the last two residents and will be moving in September, 1999. Keota lost its incorporated status in 1990. There were four different newspapers at four different times from 1908-1975. The last operating post office closed in 1890. The school foundation is still there and was established in 1888 and closed in sometime in the 1930's.

Patton – Bounty Hunter – 7th Adventure

Granite, Colorado

Coordinates: 39°02′38″N 106°15′44″W - The Pike's Peak Gold Rush that began in 1859 brought an unprecedented number of people into the Colorado Territory. Among the earliest gold discoveries in Colorado were placer deposits near the headwaters of the Arkansas River in Oro city. In 1860, Cache Creek, a mining camp near Granite, became the first settlement of note with a population of about 300. By the following year, Granite, located on either side of the Arkansas River, exploded to a population of 3,000. The settlement included a three-mile stretch of river and extended two-miles up Cache Creek. In 1867 free quartz gold was discovered and a mill was built. In 1868 the county seat was moved to Granite from the neighboring town of Dayton near present-day Twin Lakes, no longer in existence. 1874 and 1875 brought the "Lake County War", a war involving a group of men from the nearby town of Nathrop known as "The Regulators", to Granite. The war reached its climax when members of the "Committee of Safety" killed Probate Judge Elias Dyer, the son of the well-known minister John Lewis Dyer, in his own courtroom. The vigilante committee had been trying to rid the county of "lawbreakers" using illegal arrests, coerced confessions and forced exile as tools in its campaign. No one was ever convicted of Judge Dyer's murder. Murders were common, but convictions were not. More than one hundred homicides occurred during this period without a single conviction; it was almost impossible to get witnesses to swear to the killings. The early prospectors included Horace Tabor, who later moved up the valley to Leadville where he was to find his fortune in the Colorado Silver Boom that swept Leadville in 1879. In a much-publicized scandal Tabor divorced his wife and married young and beautiful Elizabeth "Baby Doe" McCourt, twenty years his junior. The Tabors had two children, Lily and Silver Dollar. They lost their wealth when the price of silver dropped in 1893 and Tabor died in 1899 with a final request of Baby Doe that she maintain the claim to their silver mine. Baby

Doe lived in squalid conditions in the tool shed of the mine for thirty years and was found dead in 1936. Until 1879 the village of Granite was located in Lake County, once one of the two largest of the Colorado Territory's original 17 counties. As the site of some of the richest placer gold strikes in Lake County, Granite held the position of county seat, but in 1878 they lost out to booming silver-rich Leadville, 17 miles to the north. However, Granite did manage to remain the county seat, but not of Lake County. They redrew the county lines creating Chaffee County, with Granite as the county seat. But a year later an election was held resulting in a win for Buena Vista, 17 miles to the south of Granite, with 1,128 votes out of a total population of 1,200 (when women couldn't vote). Granite declared the election fraudulent and refused to give up its position, so late one night a group of men from Buena Vista took matters into their own hands.

Mount Oxford, Colorado
Coordinates 38°57′53″N 106°20′20″W - is a high mountain summit of the Collegiate Peaks in the Sawatch Range of the Rocky Mountains of North America. The 14,160-foot fourteener is located in the Collegiate Peaks Wilderness of San Isabel National Forest. The mountain was named in honor of the University of Oxford.

West Buffalo Peak – Coordinates 38°59′30″N
106°07′30″W - Elevation 13,327 ft. is a summit in the Mosquito Range of central Colorado. The mountain is the highest peak of the Buffalo Peaks, slightly taller than East Buffalo Peak. It is located in the Buffalo Peaks Wilderness.

Kurt James thrilling western The Keegan Trail Sample:

CHAPTER 1

We were pushing the horses hard trying to stay ahead of those Redlegs, but they were tiring fast and there was not much left in them. We were going to have to find a place suitable to make a stand before both horses gave up. I had never run a horse to death and I was not about to start now. My three-year-old mare "Sammy" which was short for Samantha was just about done for. Sandy's horse named "Horse" was just as bad as shape as mine.

Looking back over my shoulder I could see the former Union soldier named Captain John Merna and two of the others 5 lift their Winchesters to their shoulders to fire even more 44 slugs in our direction. Even though more than 10 years had passed since the end of the Civil War and these bastards were still hunting down anyone with a Missouri accent. No wonder it was called Bloody Kansas before and during the war. I hate Kansas.

Feeling the heat and hearing the air sing as one of those 44 slugs split the air by my head, I was thankful that those union boys could never hit anything firing from horseback. That being said that last one was a tad close for comfort. Way too close.

Sandy started to cross at a full gallop in front of me, forcing Sammy and myself to make the turn with him. Just as I was just about to give him the ole' stink eye, he pointed to an old farm house. A wooden one instead of a sod house. I would have preferred a sod house because they stop bullets better and not much to burn except maybe part of the roof.

Feeling Sammy stumble and almost go down told me that the old wooden farm house just in front of us and a couple of miles east of Dighton Kansas would have to do.

Glancing at Sandy I shook my head up and down in a "yes" motion indicating to my best friend that I understood as he took point as we headed to the old abandon house.

With Captain Merna and the other 5 Redlegs not more than a 100 yards behind us I glanced at Sandy, knowing he knew the drill and would grab all of his weapons and what ammo he had as soon as we dismounted. Near death experiences and fighting Union Redlegs was not new to us seeing how we had fought on the southern side of the War Between the States.

Both Sandy and I pulled hard back on our reins and dismounted on the run with a practiced maneuver. Almost with the same motion of pulling my Winchester from its scabbard and slapping Sammy on her left hind quarters to send her galloping away, I made fast tracks toward the door of the old house hoping that the door was not locked or barred in some way.

Sandy has been always a tad faster than me on his feet and got to the door before me and with no time to see if it was indeed locked, he gave it a heavy kick with his boot and the door sprung open as we both piled in as three 44 slugs splintered the door frame. I quickly moved to my left and slammed the door shut as two more slugs hit the door and the last one ricocheted off to parts unknown.

Using my lever action I jacked a 44 shell into the firing breech of my rifle and found an open window and let loose two rounds in quick succession in the general direction of those Kansas Redleg boys to keep them honest and ducking their heads.

The midsummer dust was still swirling in the air as John Merna and his boys dismounted in a hurry and slapping their horse to scatter them so they would not get accidentally shot. Sandy fired a couple of shots in their direction as well before he said, "Do you believe it Mac? It has been over 10 years and those boys still wear them damn red leggings. I still cannot imagine being that mad about the little ole' Civil War. Remind me again my friend - who won the war?"

Firing and missing once at an exposed leg stuck out from behind an old wagon about 70 feet out I started to laugh at Sandy, "They won Sandy, and we lost."

Looking at me with a smile stretched from ear to ear, he replied, "I just don't get it why they are still mad! You and I have not worn any gray except trail dust since before Robert E. Lee gave up his saber."

Sitting down with my back against the front wall I was thankful for whoever had built this house was a fine carpenter because none of those 44 slugs seemed to make any holes in the wood siding.

Since Captain Merna and his Redleg boys quit firing at the house realizing it was not doing any good I took the time to ponder a few things. The house, as I had already determined was abandoned, but well built. Not one piece of furniture was left and the one room house was completely empty except for Sandy and myself. The broad glass windows had long ago succumbed to the Kansas summer heat and the winter cold and were cracked and broken. We could defend this place for a long spell if Merna and his boys didn't set it afire. Of course, those Redlegs were always setting things on fire during the war. I guess it was not a question of if, just a question of when. Just a matter of timing is all.

Sandy was taking this lull in the action to eat some venison jerky as he glanced out the window from time to time to keep tabs on Captain Merna and his band of misfits. He of course had a huge smile on his face.

Ron "Sandy" Sands had always been my best friend growing up. Women seemed to find him handsome with a 6'2'' solidly built frame. He was built like his father and could move like the wind. His hair was dark and most of the time he let it grow long until it was lying on his shoulders. He tried to keep his face clean shaven when we had adequate water available to shave thinking the ladies liked him better that way. He was a dead shot with any rifle and a fair shot with his Colt pistol. Then there was his constant smile. Even in the heat of battle, he was always smiling and never seemed to be bothered much by the bullets being flung around him. He was one of a kind that's for sure. He was a good and decent man and I could have not asked for a better best friend.

Sandy always called me "Mac" even though my name was McCall Patton. Sandy and I were roughly the same build except I had larger hands, which is what Sandy always said was the reason I was such a fast draw with my Colt pistol. My hair was dark like Sandy's hair, but I like to keep it short and tidy like my Ma always liked it. Most folks that we ran across just assumed we were brothers, since we looked so much alike.

We both grew up in Clay County in Western Missouri and some folks called Clay County "Little Dixie" and it was also home of Frank and Jesse James who were my 2nd or 3rd cousins. I could never remember which.

Missouri back during the Civil War was a border state and some fought for the Union, but most fought for the south. Coming from an area called "Little Dixie" Sandy and I ended up on the southern side of the conflict. It was in our blood and most of our kin fought for the "Missouri Bushwhackers" as did we. The Kansas and Missouri border became a battle field all on its own that most of the time had nothing to do with the real reasons which brought about the Civil War. We fought the Kansas "Jayhawkers" and of course the "Redlegs" which were Union forces even if they were never recognized by the U.S. Government. Captain John Merna and this bunch were the worst of the worst.

Even though Sandy and I were not part of the raid on Lawrence, Kansas that massacred more than 200 people by Quantrill's Raiders, whose band consisted of a lot of the same folks we fought alongside with. Sandy and I were disgusted at what transpired that day and left the fighting behind and went home to work our farms with our families. It was back home is where I had my first run in with Captain Merna.

At the end of the Civil War Captain Merna and his brother Bob and a bunch of renegade Redlegs raided into Clay County hoping to find Frank and Jesse James. Of course they never found Frank or Jesse, but they burned the home I grew up in to the ground after killing my folks in an all-out pitched battle. I was able to escape and the very next day with the help of my best friend Sandy was able to track down and kill Bob Merna and two other Redlegs in a shoot-out in the back woods. I considered the score even and settled. Captain Merna had a different thought and had always hated me for killing his brother that day.

Even though I had never forgotten what John Merna looked like I never again saw him until yesterday in Alamota, Kansas which was southeast of Dighton and is a station and shipping point for a division of the Atchison, Topeka and Santa Fe Railway. He was alone at the time and we had a few words as Sandy and I bought some supplies for the trail heading to Colorado. At the time I saw no harm in letting him go about his business since the war had long been over. I had no idea he had 5 other former Redlegs traveling with him. Merna and his outlaw Redlegs jumped us this morning hoping to kill us on the plains where there would be no witness to their act of murder.

Sandy lifted his Winchester and said, heads up Mac we got a brave soul heading this way on his horse with a flaming torch. They mean to set us afire!"

AUTHOR'S NOTE

It is my hope you have found Colorado to be a living and breathing character as much as Dale, Jeb, Cinders - I love Colorado and everything it offers.

I also wanted to assure you that the Colorado geography, along the path my hero Dale Lee Patton and his Australian dingo Jeb traveled through the Colorado Mountains, does in fact exist - every mountain, mountain range, mountain pass, town, mining camp, river, and creek.

I took some liberty in using the modern names in some cases or the more historical names if I thought it fit the story better. I wanted folks who were locals or familiar with this Colorado area to be able to follow along on Dale and Jeb's adventure more easily in their mind and to be able to travel if they wanted to on horseback, foot, or even by car or 4 wheel drive the same path of Dale Lee Patton in his quest for retribution.

.

ABOUT THE AUTHOR

Kurt James was born and raised in the foothills of the Colorado Rocky Mountains. With family roots in western Kansas and having lived in South Dakota for 20 years Kurt naturally had become an old western and nature enthusiast. Over the years Kurt has become one of Colorado's prominent nature photographer's through his brand name of Midnight Wind Photography. His poetry has been featured in the Denver Post, PM Magazine and on 9NEWS in Denver, Colorado. Kurt is also a feature writer for HubPages and Creative Exiles with the article's focused on Colorado history, ghost towns, outlaws, and poetry. Inspired at a young age by writers such as Jack London, Louis L'Amour and Max Brand have formed Kurt's natural ability as a storyteller. Kurt has published 5 novels all based in and around the Colorado Rocky Mountains. Using the Midnight Wind Publishing brand Kurt has also released a poetry collection - Poetry and Thoughts of a Wandering Man - (Uniquely Colorado edition) and now this collection - Poetry and Reflections of a Wandering Man (Random Thoughts edition) all are available in print or download on Amazon, Barnes and Noble, Goodreads and other fine bookstores. And a few shady bookstores as well. Kurt is working on his 7th Colorado adventure tale novel "When the Song Vanishes".

Kurt James

Colorado Storyteller